The Cats

Karen Anne Golden

Copyright

This book or eBook is a work of fiction. Names, characters, places and incidents are products of the author's imagination or are used fictitiously. Any resemblance to actual events, locales, persons or cats, living or dead, is entirely coincidental.

Edited by Vicki Braun

Book cover concept by Karen Anne Golden

Book cover design by philipsinc, Fiverr.com

ISBN-13: 978-1523632367

ISBN-10: 1523632364

Dedication

To

My Sister Linda

Table of Contents

Prologue

It was getting dark. Katherine paced the floor in front of the pink mansion's parlor window. Scout and Abra, two seal-point Siamese sisters, were sitting on the windowsill, watching the snow fall.

Moving over to the cats, Katherine petted their backs. "When is this snow ever going to stop?"

"Raw," Abra cried in a sweet voice. She nuzzled her head against Katherine's arm.

Looking out the window, Scout suddenly began to growl; Abra did the same. They stood up on their hind legs and dangled their front paws, doing their meerkat pose. Scout began wildly sniffing the air.

"What's wrong?" Katherine asked.

Scout cried a mournful "waugh." It sounded like a warning.

Staring out the window, Katherine saw a figure slide and stumble on the sidewalk. It fell down and then slowly got back up.

"Why on earth is someone taking a walk in this weather?" she asked out loud. "Cats, I've got to go outside and see if this person needs help."

Scout leaped down from the sill and threw herself against Katherine.

"Scout, what's the matter with you? I have to do this. I'll only be gone a minute."

"Na-waugh," Scout pleaded.

"Take Abra and go upstairs."

"Rawww," Abra cried in a plaintive wail.

Katherine gently pushed Scout aside. She ran to the front door and opened it. A woman fell in and collapsed on the floor. Blood was flowing from underneath her coat.

"Oh, you poor thing. What happened to you?"

"Shot," the woman gasped. "Shut . . . "

Katherine closed the door and locked it. She grabbed her cell and punched in 911. "This is Katherine Cokenberger. Send an ambulance to my house. A woman has been shot."

Ending the call, she stooped down and spoke softly to the prone woman. "Who did this to you?"

The woman struggled to breathe, and whispered something.

"What did you say?"

"Run. Get out of the house."

Chapter One

Five months after the explosion of a water heater damaged the pink mansion, twenty-eight-year-old millionaire, Katherine Kendall Cokenberger — AKA Katz — and her new husband, Jake, moved their family of seven cats back into their beloved home. During the five-month restoration, the family lived in a red brick bungalow built in 1912. Katherine had bought the bungalow as a guest house. At the time, she didn't know how handy a second home would prove to be.

After the explosion, Katherine was reluctant to move from the mansion, but the fire inspector said it wasn't safe to live there. He wisely suggested several reasons that Jake, the cats, and she live elsewhere while the mansion was being repaired: Dust, noise, and the constant in-and-out of several construction workers.

Katherine kept a careful eye on the renovations, especially her basement-level classroom. She taught a free computer course to select townspeople to help them get better-paying jobs. Handyman Cokey, Jake's uncle, was in charge of the window replacement on the back side of the house and the installation of new appliances in the basement. A state-of-the art water heater was installed to replace the one Cokey had blown up when he left flammable rags in the vicinity of its pilot light. Because he felt responsible for what happened and counted his lucky stars that no one was killed in the blast, he provided his services free-of-charge. Cokey's wife, Margie, a pro at restoring older homes, removed damaged wallpaper and lovingly re-papered several rooms in the classic Victorian style, using hand-printed papers made by a company based in San Francisco — the great city of "painted lady" Victorian homes.

Jake's and Katherine's first night back in the mansion was a difficult ordeal. The cats didn't want to settle down. Katherine thought that by midnight, they would tire of chasing each other up and down the stairs or playing with their fake mice toys. The couple found it impossible to fall asleep because the hyperactive cats kept waking them up. When Jake called "time out" and locked the cats in their playroom, the cats pitched a royal conniption fit — shrieking at the top of their lungs, throwing themselves against the closed door, or pretending to fight, which brought the concerned humans to check whether they were dead or alive. From the sounds of the fake battles, it would be easy for a non-cat person to assume the worst.

Earlier, Katherine and Jake had chosen to stay in the guest bedroom. The newly purchased furniture for their new master bedroom, in the front of the house, hadn't arrived, so the couple slept in the bedroom with the massive Victorian renaissance-revival furniture. Jake referred to it as the chunky monkey suite. The tall headboard was the perfect perch for Lilac and Abby, who were not content to stay put, and took turns climbing up, and then leaping off, sometimes using Jake or Katherine as a springboard to the floor below. The new kitten Crowie didn't want to be away from his furry friends, so he attempted to climb the headboard, but was thwarted by the fact that it would only comfortably seat two cats, not three.

Scout and Abra prowled the house, doing their reconnaissance mission, loudly vocalizing their Siamese reports so they could be heard by members of the house, and probably by the neighboring households, as well. They'd start on the first floor, then work their way up to Jake's and Katherine's room, where they'd wail their findings, then start all over again.

Shutting the door to the masked duo and keeping it closed was impossible, because just as the couple dozed off, Scout and Abra would take turns pawing at the door, jumping up to hit the door knob, and then worked as a team to open the door. Scout would clutch the knob while Abra pulled the door open. The former magician's show cats were highly skilled at opening doors, even locked ones.

The only cats oblivious to the noisy torment was the adorable blue-eyed Iris, affectionately known as Miss Siam, and her soulmate, kitten Dewey, who had the meow of an opera baritone. They curled up at the foot of the bed, and hissed at any cat that woke them up.

Half-asleep, and imagining a giant anaconda was choking her, Katherine woke up to a warm, breathing creature draped across her neck. "Scout, I can't breathe," she complained to the Siamese, who had finally exhausted herself by collapsing in bed.

"Waugh," Scout protested, not moving.

Jake rolled over and said sleepily, "Scout, you're strangling your mama."

Scout reluctantly moved to Abra and began washing Abra's pointed ears. Abra crossed her eyes dreamily.

Abby, Lilac, and Crowie were underneath the blankets, burrowed to the bottom of the bed, while Iris and Dewey were wrapped together in a breathing fur ball on Katherine's side.

"Mao," Dewey bellowed in his booming Siamese voice. Iris bopped him on the head with her paw to quiet the kitten.

Katherine giggled.

"What's so funny, Sweet Pea?" Jake asked lovingly.

"Oh, sleeping on this antique bed with the nine of us, counting the cats, vying for a position on a full-size mattress . . . I was just thinking how happy I am."

"I'm looking forward to the new king-size mattress. Then there'll be plenty of room," Jake said, yawning.

Katherine squeezed his arm affectionately. "I'm so tired. Maybe we should stay in bed all day. It's so warm and toasty here. It's freezing in this house."

"That's because it's freezing outside. When you get dressed, you'll feel warmer if you bundle up in layers, because today is the day we make snow angels."

"What's a snow angel?" Katherine asked, baffled.

"It's a Cokenberger family tradition. Right after a big snow, before anyone has stomped around and messed it up, you go outside and lie down . . . "

"Lie down? In the snow? Are you crazy?"

"You bundle up first," he explained in a matter-of-fact tone. "You find an undisturbed place, and lie down with your arms and legs outstretched. Then you sweep your arms and legs back and forth, creating a depression in the snow. When you're done, the snow angel appears."

"You've got to be kidding me. My family in Brooklyn didn't have this tradition."

"That's because in your neck of the woods there's cement all around and it would be hard to find a spot for the angel."

"Not necessarily. There are parts of Brooklyn that aren't under concrete."

"We've got to make our angels before the snow flies," Jake continued.

"Before the snow flies? I think it's already flown. There's at least a foot of snow out there."

"Flown or not, according to the Guinness World Records, North Dakota holds the world record for the most snow angels made in one particular place — a whopping 8,000-something."

"How about we not beat North Dakota's record and stay in bed."

Jake ignored the comment. "Hey, wouldn't it be fun if Daryl and Colleen could join us?"

"Join us where?"

"At Chester's Snow Angel Farm."

"Where is that?"

"A few miles from here."

Katherine laughed out loud. "Colleen hates the cold. I couldn't imagine her making a snow angel. Besides, Daryl is probably very busy with his deputy duties."

"Okay, maybe it's a Jake and Katz event. Oh, by the way, Chester's daughter operates a hot chocolate bar."

"Hot chocolate?" Katherine said, perking up to the idea of a cup of her favorite winter beverage.

"Yes, her specialty is peppermint loaded with marshmallows."

"You're killing me," she said in a teasing voice.

"Since I've solved our problem of what to do on this official university snow day, I'm off to find another blanket for the bed. Where's the feather comforter my parents gave us for a wedding present?"

Before she could answer, Abby tunneled up from the covers until her head peeked out, "Chirp," she cried. She reached out and patted Katherine with her paw.

"Try the bottom drawer in the oak dresser in the guest room," Katherine called after him, then whispered to Abigail — the Abyssinian with a propensity to eat wool, polyester, and goose feathers. "I think your secret is no longer safe."

The nonplussed feline blinked her golden eyes and ran her tongue over her lips.

"You didn't just do that," Katherine said with a twinkle in her eye.

Jake returned to the room and spread the blanket on the bed. His voice rose with shock. "What is that?" he said, pointing to a gaping hole the size of a Frisbee in the middle of the comforter.

"What do you mean?" Katherine asked innocently.

"Chirp," Abby cried, gazing up at Jake with love in her eyes.

"I know we don't have moths," Jake said, amused, picking up Abby, who collapsed in his arms. He turned her on her back and ran his hand over her stomach. She purred loudly.

"What are we going to tell your Mom and Dad?"

"They're not coming back from Florida until spring, so I think we'll come up with something by then."

Jake climbed back in bed and put his cold feet on Katherine's leg.

"Stop it!" she said, half-serious, half-laughing. "Your feet are glacial!"

"Katz, I've got it figured out this way. The mansion is over a hundred-years-old. It's not insulated. The windows are single-pane, and the house is about as energy efficient as a tent in the artic."

"But, Jake," Katherine said, concerned, turning toward him. "We could have stayed at the bungalow. At least it was warm."

"I don't know about you, but I felt . . ." He didn't finish the sentence.

"Felt what?" Katherine coaxed.

"It wouldn't be cool to not move back when so many people fixed up the mansion to the way she was before your friend, Jacky —"

"Oh, here we go," Katherine complained.

"Let me finish. Before Jacky decided to come late to our wedding, drunker than a skunk, and then have a smoke, which blew up the water heater!"

"Ma-waugh," Scout agreed.

"Jake, you're never going to let that go, are you?"

"Nope," he said, then added, "A house of this age shouldn't be left vacant in the winter."

"That's what you keep telling me," Katherine said, starting to get up.

Jake gently pulled her back. "What's the hurry, Mrs. Cokenberger?"

"Suddenly, I'm starving. I can fix us a three-cheese omelet."

"That's one of the reasons why I married you," Jake chuckled.

"You are really full of it this morning. You know I can't cook."

"Yowl," Iris agreed. The other cats responded likewise. Lilac burrowed out from underneath the blankets, and stood on Jake's chest. "Me-yowl," Lilac shrieked. Abby chirped in a low tone.

"Oops, I guess I should have spelled it out."

"Cats don't eat omelets . . . or do they?"

"They do if they have t-u-n-a," she spelled, "in them."

"Okay, last one out of bed gets to shovel the front walk."

As if on cue, the cats soared off the bed, and thundered down the hall. Racing down the stairs, Scout cried up to the humans who were slowly taking their time getting out of bed. "Waugh," she demanded, which sounded like, "Feed me. I'm starving to death."

* * *

After the cats had been fed, and Jake had finished his fourth cup of coffee, he reached across the table for Katherine's hand. "I have a great idea where my new office will be."

Katherine looked at him curiously. "It's in the basement. Are you not happy down there?"

Jake gave a curious look. "Actually, Katz, I'm not a superstitious kind of guy, but since the judge died there, I

17

can't get past it. I can't concentrate. The place gives me the creeps."

"I had no idea. Why don't you make one of the bedrooms upstairs into your office?"

"That's exactly what I want to do, but it won't be in one of the bedrooms."

"Where's it going to be?"

"In the attic."

Katherine spit out her coffee. "The attic?" she asked incredulously. "Jake, it's an architectural nightmare up there. It would involve major remodeling. Besides, it's full of bats."

"Seeing one bat every year doesn't qualify as being full of bats."

"But it doesn't have interior walls or a ceiling. The floorboards need work."

"Uncle Cokey and I'll sand the floorboards, and then stain them."

"No way! Cokey and flammable stain are not allowed in this house."

"Understood. Now, if you're finished eating, come with me to your office. I have some sketches of the floorplan to show you."

Katherine smiled and looked at him adoringly. She loved him. She'd give him the moon if she could.

Chapter Two

Stevie Sanders, the son of Erie's crime boss, pulled his new red Dodge Ram into a parking space outside the Dew Drop Inn, a tavern owned by his father, Sam. Stevie had been estranged from his dad for several months, when he refused to partake in any more of his dad's illegal transactions. Sam's businesses ranged from operating a house of ill repute in the trailer court he owned outside town limits, to drug trafficking across state lines. The latter involved a network of backwoods boys who "cooked" meth, and other more sophisticated criminals who smuggled drugs throughout the Midwest.

Turning off the ignition, Stevie scanned the near-empty parking lot and recognized three of the vehicles parked in the gravel: a Toyota Tundra pickup belonging to his father, bartender Eddie's beat-up 1995 Saturn, and the rusted Jeep Cherokee of Stevie's older half-brother, Dave. Stevie wondered why Dave, who had gone "clean" long before he had, was at the Dew Drop Inn.

Stevie got out and headed into the deserted bar. It took him a moment to adjust his eyes to the dimly lit tavern. Typically, the place was the best jukin' joint in Erie, but at three o'clock in the afternoon, only two men sat at the bar, while Eddie took care of them. His dad sat on one of the bar stools, busy counting money. Dave was nursing his beer and staring blankly into the bar's mirror. Eddie looked at Stevie warily.

"Dad," Stevie said, stepping over and taking the stool next to his drug-dealing father. He nodded at his brother. "Dave, how's it goin'?"

"Just fine, bro. What brings ya this way?"

"I can ask you the same."

Dave didn't answer.

Sam Sanders didn't look up, but continued counting. "What can I do you for?" he asked in a disinterested voice.

"Well to start with — "

The bartender interrupted. "What can I git ya?"

"Bring me a Coke, but none of that diet stuff."

"That's a sissy drink," Sam said. "I've got some mighty fine tequila. Why don't you have a shot of that? It'll take the edge off."

"I'm workin' today."

The bartender tipped his head back and laughed. "Why don't ya have a pint of Guinness like that Irish feller was drinkin' a few months back. The way he was beltin' 'em down, I'd say that's a mighty good beer."

Stevie shot him a dirty look. "That Irish feller caused an explosion at Katherine Kendall's place. He told the cops someone here was buyin' him drinks. Was that you, Dad?"

"Guilty," Sam said, holding up one hand. "I figured I was doing you a favor."

"How's that?" Stevie asked suspiciously.

"He was spoutin' off about crashing the wedding. It seems he had some kind of fling with Ms. Kendall."

"That ain't true," Stevie fired off angrily.

"Hold on there, spitfire. I didn't mean any disrespect. I heard how that woman got you out of going back to jail."

"Dad, I didn't come here to talk about Mrs. Cokenberger."

"Oh, yeah, that's right. The wedding went on. How unfortunate for you," Sam said cynically. "My gut tells me you like this Kendall woman big-time. If you ever want me to *do* something about that Jake guy, just say the word — "

Stevie cut him off. "Ain't necessary. I've never had trouble gittin' a woman, but killin' her husband ain't gonna cut it with me," he said, then changed the subject. "I'm here because I'm tryin' to find Darlene."

"What do you want with your ex-wife?" Sam asked, his face clouding. He moved the metal cash box full of money aside, and for the first time, looked at his son. "What the hell's going on?" he demanded. "You've been divorced for a good ten years, and now you're looking to find her. Why would you think that I know where she is?"

"Because she buys dope from you."

Sam snickered. "Like I sell dope to all my customers. Son, you got it wrong. My associates sell it to her."

Stevie glared. "I went over to Darlene's trailer, and someone else is livin' in it. She didn't know where Darlene was. I've got to find her 'cause I want to see my daughter."

"Get a lawyer," Sam said, then added, "According to your ex, you ain't paid child support in a long time."

"I ain't paid support because I can't find her."

"All right, I'll stop jerkin' you around. I know where she is. She went back to Kentucky to live with her mama; took Salina with her. They came in asking for money, and a little pick-me-up."

"What do you mean, *they*? Darlene brought Salina in here?"

"No, son, pay attention. Darlene came in here with this beefy looking guy. Salina was outside in the car."

Dave, who had been quietly hanging on to every word, added, "Darlene's been livin' with this guy down by the tracks. Don't know his name. Just sayin', your ex has a serious meth problem."

Sam said, amused, "She should change her name to Crystal."

"Not funny," Stevie snapped. "Why didn't you call me? And, you Dave, what's your excuse? I don't want my daughter livin' with a meth head."

"Well, son, I'll put it to you gently. No court's gonna give you custody of your daughter when you've got a prison record. Besides, I didn't call because I figured you didn't want to talk to me anymore. That's what you said, ain't it, son?"

Stevie's jaw hardened. "Does Darlene's mama still live at the same address?"

"Yep."

"I'm gonna go git my daughter." Stevie grabbed his coat and started to leave.

"I wouldn't drive in this weather. Hell, you can get out of Indiana, but once you hit the holler where she lives, you'll be neck-deep in snow. And I'm not talking about that stuff falling from the sky."

Stevie headed to the door, then turned. He started to say something, then changed his mind. He opened the door and began to leave.

Sam called him back. "Wait. You can't go down there without protection." He pulled a handgun from his hip holster and handed it to his son. "The law can't trace it. Ditch it if you have to use it."

Stevie nodded, then left, tucking the gun in the back of his jeans.

Dave slid off his bar stool. "Wait, Stevie. Give the gun back. You don't want to appear before the parole board again. I'm comin' with. I've got a license to carry."

Stevie made a face, reluctantly handed the gun back to his father, and turned to Dave, "Yeah, you're right. I don't want to do anything stupid."

"You wanna drive or me?" Dave asked.

Stevie raised his brow. "I think I'll drive. Besides, you haven't seen my new truck."

"Let me git my coat."

"You boys take care now," Sam said, moving the cash box back in front of him. He resumed counting.

Chapter Three

Madison Orson, an attractive woman in her late twenties — a blond, blue-eyed former model — sat at a secure reception desk located in the front room of a premier Manhattan jewelry store. A sliding, bullet-proof window enabled her to greet customers, receive and send mail, and perform a number of other tasks included in her receptionist duties.

Behind Madison was a full glass wall, to which she could turn in awe and admire the many display cases filled with expensive jewelry. Four impeccably dressed salesmen manned each of four counters. Madison loved watching them. To her, they were eye candy or future prey, depending on her mood or her plans to leave Manhattan. But for now, Madison was solely interested in the tall, handsome Russian who was the daytime security guard. She caught him looking at her. She smiled seductively and then turned to face her computer screen. She checked her watch, and noticed the time. *Where is he*, she thought irritably. *He should have been here an hour ago.*

Madison's reception skills were outstanding, and she had an excellent work record to prove it. The owner of the store, middle-aged Nikolai Zhukov, was very impressed, and had contacted the temporary agency where she worked and asked if they would release Madison from her contract, so she could work for him full-time. The agency was slow in responding because Madison was an asset to its firm, and she would be hard to replace.

When Madison was in her early twenties, she worked for a renown modeling agency, commanding a high salary. She modeled in fashion shows, did magazine shoots, and had several walk-on roles in the movies. But those jobs dried up when younger, thinner women were hired to replace the slightly older ones. And years of cocaine abuse had not been kind to her skin. It was a cutthroat world, but she missed the adrenaline rush. Now she could hardly make ends meet working temporary reception jobs that usually ended before she'd had time to call her desk her own. She was surprised her current one had lasted over a month. She'd landed an utopian job in more ways than one.

Madison snapped out of her reverie. A mailman in his fifties, who had too much to drink the night before, came in wheeling his one-handled cart. Madison had been grooming him to trust her by using her gorgeous looks as a tool. She instantly turned on the charm. "Hello, Mike. How are you today? Did you catch the Knicks game last night?"

Mike looked her up and down. "Good morning, sunshine. Yes, I had great seats. There's a game coming up. Wanna watch it from the sports bar down the street?"

"I'd love to," she smiled. "First round is on me," she said.

A prospective customer walked into the store. Madison assumed her professional stance, as did Mike.

"I'll be with you in a moment," she said to the well-attired woman with diamonds as big as the Ritz in each ear.

"I have an appointment," the woman said impatiently, with her nose stuck up in the air.

Madison was taken aback for a moment, then looked at her computer screen. "Name?" she asked, scanning the day's calendar.

"Courtney Hughes."

"Here you are. Mr. Zhukov is expecting you. I'll buzz you in," Madison said sweetly, ignoring the fact that the woman never once established eye contact with her. She reached underneath her keyboard drawer and pressed the button. Courtney walked in and was instantly greeted by Mr. Zhukov, who grabbed the woman's hand and kissed it.

Madison rolled her eyes. *Vultures*, she thought.

Mike said, "Penny for your thoughts."

She lowered her thick, dark lashes, then looked up. "My thoughts are worth more than that."

"I'd love to find out," Mike flirted. "Listen, I have a package that requires your signature."

Madison gave a cursory glance at the brown-papered package. "My signature? Are you sure? Normally Mr. Zhukov signs for parcels."

The mailman continued holding the package. "Do you want it or not?" he teased.

"Of course."

"Sign here and it's all yours."

"Got it," she said, signing.

The mailman passed the package through the opening in the glass. Madison took it and studied the return address, then laughed.

"I guess it wouldn't be professional for me to ask who it's from?" Mike asked coyly.

Madison shook her head, then said dismissively. "Text me later about the Knicks game, okay?"

The mailman understood his cue to leave, so he wheeled his cart out of the jewelry store, turning around to check out the stunning ex-model one more time.

Madison wasn't looking. Instead, she had picked up her cell, and was now talking animatedly into it.

Chapter Four

Jake drove several miles north on US 41, and turned onto a snow-covered road. He reached down on the floorboard, between the seats, and pulled down the lever for four-wheel drive. A snow plow had recently gone through, pushing the snow to the side of the road and creating a bank several feet high.

Katherine was riding in the passenger seat. "We should have taken the Subaru," she worried. "You don't have to slow down, reach down to get it to do its thing."

"The Jeep's doing fine. You shouldn't say things that will hurt its feelings."

"Should I be jealous?" she joked. "How far is the farm?"

"A little ways down yonder," Jake said, faking a thick country accent.

Katherine reached in her bag and took out her cell. She tapped the weather app, but her screen remained blank.

"I should have checked the weather site online before we left. I can't get a signal out here."

"Yep, deep in the boonies," he continued with his accent. "I checked your computer monitor before we left," he offered mysteriously.

"Why?" she asked with an inquisitive look, her brows furrowed.

"To make sure the cats hadn't surfed up any clues that might warn us about something."

"Like what?"

"Oh, like we'd be caught in a blizzard and have to stay in the Jeep for a few days."

Katherine was amused at the direction the conversation was heading, and rolled with it. "And maybe we should have brought some blankets, snacks, and something to drink so we wouldn't end up like the Donner party. Well, what did the cats surf up?"

"That's for the cats and me to know."

35

"That's my line."

Jake laughed. "I'm just messin' with you. The cats didn't surf up anything. But why the desktop background of an island beach? I haven't seen that one before."

"It's psychological. When I look at it, I think warm thoughts —"

"Then you should have a picture of me," Jake teased.

"No, silly, I'm thinking warm thoughts because I'm literally freezing in our house."

Jake hit a large chunk of ice, and the Jeep skidded to the left. He quickly played the steering wheel, and drove out of the skid. "Whoa," he said. "That was a close one."

Katherine clutched the Jeep's passenger-side grab bar. "Be careful."

"Chester's farm isn't far."

"There's the sign," Katherine pointed, relieved they were almost there. The large billboard was mounted on two rustic posts, and seemed out-of-place in the snow covered field. She laughed out loud. 'Chester's Snow Angel Farm. Let's make Erie, Indiana, the snow angel capital — one angel at a time.'"

Jake turned in and drove down a narrow country lane into a parking lot crowded with pickup trucks. A ramshackle kiosk served as the office with two people standing inside behind a counter: an elderly man with a fur-lined cap and matching parka was selling tickets, and a younger woman was serving hot chocolate. Several people were lined up for the cocoa. Katherine made a beeline for the queue, while Jake did business with the man.

"How ya doin', Chester?" he asked. "What do you think about this weather?" In Indiana, polite conversation usually started with a question about the weather.

"Snow comin' down pretty hard, if ya ask me. If it keeps this up, we could get a big one."

"You mean blizzard?"

"Yep, if the wind kicks up. But for right now, the snow is a light and powdery, which is good for the angels."

"I see you've got the plots staked out this year," Jake said, looking at the orange grid of plastic stakes marking off each angel section. A long wooden platform, topped by a railing, stood south of the staked plots. A few parents stood on the platform to take photos of their angel-making children. "I admire how scientific you are," he added.

"Yep, gotta put Indiana on the map. So far we have three hundred and fifty-three angels. I hope the weather doesn't keep folks from comin'."

"How's your daughter doing in school?" Jake inquired, looking over at the young woman serving steaming cocoa to Katz, who was grinning ear-to-ear.

"Doin' fine. You know, she just got a letter in the mail. Seems she's been selected to take your wife's computer class come March."

"No, I didn't know that. Great."

"Okay then, Jake," Chester said, taking Jake's money. "The Cokenberger section is over yonder with the red ties on it. You just missed Cokey, Margie, and the kids. Your grandpa was just here, too, but your grandma stayed home this year."

"Maybe my grandfather should have stayed at home with her. I admire him for braving the cold."

Chester nodded, then came out from behind the counter and took Jake by the arm. He led him a few feet from the kiosk so that what he had to say would be out of earshot from the other customers. "Did you hear who bought the tract of land across from me?" he asked, whispering.

Jake answered in a low voice. "No. I know it's been for sale for a while."

"Sam Sanders."

"You don't say," Jake said, surprised.

"Yeppers, he's gonna start a windmill farm."

"Wow, maybe that's a good thing."

"You know that man is a crook, right?"

Jake shrugged, but didn't answer. He left gossiping duties to other nosy Erie townspeople down at the diner.

"Well, I gotta say," Chester continued. "He keeps the road to the old farmhouse pretty darn plowed. I think he's havin' the place fixed up, because I see a lot of trucks goin' in and out."

"Could be."

"Good to see ya, Jake," Chester said, walking toward a man who had just gotten out of an extended cab pickup.

Jake joined Katherine at the kiosk.

She handed him a Styrofoam cup of steaming hot chocolate. "Here, get warmed up before we have to go flip around in the snow," she kidded.

A middle-aged woman, carrying a digital camera, came over and spoke to the couple. "Hello, Jake. So happy to see ya. Is this the new Mrs.?"

Katherine thought, *No, she didn't just refer to me as "the new Mrs."*

"Yes, Angie, this is Katherine."

"Pleased to meet ya. I'm a friend of Jake's mom."

"Nice meeting you," Katherine said. "Are you taking photos of the event?"

"Sure am. When you're finished with your angels, make sure I get a pic of your handiwork," she said, walking away.

Jake whispered. "Sweet Pea, I saw your reaction when Angie asked if you were the new Mrs. She didn't mean anything by it."

"You mean she wasn't making a reference to your first wife?"

"No, that's just the way folks talk around here. There's a lot of Hoosier ways you need to learn." He reached over and kissed her on the cheek.

She smiled, and sipped more of her hot chocolate. In a few minutes, Jake finished his and threw the empty cup in a metal garbage can.

Katherine finished hers and did the same. "Okay, let's get a move on before we freeze to death. I feel like we're in the middle of a scene from Fargo," she kidded. "Where do we go?"

"See those red ties. They mark the Cokenberger section."

"Amazing. I had no idea this tradition existed."

"It's an Erie tradition." Jake took her by the arm and led her to the site. "I'll go first." He carefully tip-toed to the blank section of snow, then fell back.

Katherine began laughing. She couldn't stop.

Jake moved his arms and legs, then got up, careful not to make too much disturbance in the snow. He yelled at Cora's friend with the camera. "Angie, got an angel for you."

Angie trudged over and snapped the shot. "That's a beauty, Mr. Jake. Your turn, Mrs."

"Katz," Katherine answered, more sharply than she intended. "My friends call me Katz." Katherine moved to the site next to Jake's, slid on snow, and fell face forward. Leaning up, she asked, "What do I do now?"

"Fling around like a fish out of water," Jake advised, grinning.

Katherine followed the instructions, then got up, brushing the snow away from her face and hair.

Fortunately, there was no one standing on the observation platform to see the *faux pas*. Jake moved over and helped.

Angie took the picture, then said, "Can't tell if it's an angel or not, but it ain't bad, if I say so myself." She walked away before Katherine could answer.

Jake grabbed her hand, and they tromped through the snow to the Jeep. He fired up the engine, and turned up the heater. "I'm freezing," she complained, her teeth chattering. "Your heater takes forever to warm up."

Jake fished around the back of the passenger seat. He pulled up a towel. "Here, dry with this. Oh, and by the way, thanks for coming with me today."

Katherine rolled her eyes and sneezed, "No comment."

*   *   *

On the way back to Erie, close to the outskirts of town, Katherine's cell phone rang. Reaching into her bag,

44

she extracted the phone and answered it. A very excited and loud realtor was on the other end.

"Hi, Mrs. Cokenberger!" the voice shouted.

Katherine moved the cell a few inches from her ear.

"This is Lucy from the Star Realty. We've got an offer on your property."

"Which one?" Katherine asked. She had more than one house currently on the market.

"The one next door to your house."

"The yellow Foursquare? That's amazing, but I haven't signed the paperwork yet," Katherine answered.

"Please do sign it. Send it right away. And don't forget to complete the disclosure form. The buyer needs this information."

"The For Sale sign isn't even up yet. How did the buyer know about it?"

"Oh, he came to my office and was looking for a house in the historic district. Lucky me, huh?" the realtor said enthusiastically.

"Yes, definitely, but is it proper to make an offer on a house he hasn't seen?"

"Oh, but he has seen it. I just showed it to him."

"Okay," Katherine said in a tell-me-more voice. "Jake and I haven't been gone more than an hour, how could you show him the house without us seeing a vehicle parked outside?"

"By photos. He didn't want to see it. He said he was familiar with the neighborhood. Then he made an offer," Lucy said, still almost shrieking in an excited voice.

"Wonderful. Thanks so much, Lucy. Can you email the offer to me. I'll look for it when I get home. Thanks again," she said, hanging up.

Katherine turned to Jake. "Well, that's good news."

Jake answered, "I think I heard. The lungs on that woman."

Katherine laughed. "We have an offer on the Foursquare, and I haven't even finished the paperwork."

"Katz, you've been wrangling with the disclosure form for too long. There isn't a check box for ghost."

Katherine said almost inaudibly, "I hope the ghost is gone for good."

"I heard that. Katz, you have to stop worrying about that house being haunted. Katrina is gone. End of story."

"I know, but according to law, I have to tell the buyer about the haunting, at least if I'm asked. Do you think it will hurt my chances of selling the house to this buyer?" she asked, already speculating on the answer.

"Not all people believe in ghosts, so maybe you'll be lucky, and the new owner will be a skeptic like me."

Later, at the pink mansion, sitting in front of her computer, Katherine downloaded the offer and sent it to the printer.

Jake stood nearby and removed the sheet of paper. He stopped reading after the first line. "Interesting," he said, handing the document to Katherine.

Katherine's read the prospective owner's name, then her jaw dropped. "Stephen Sanders? Stevie wants to buy the house."

"Yeah, probably to keep an eye on you," Jake said suspiciously.

"Contrary to your opinion of Stevie, which isn't good, Stevie is not a stalker. He saved my life. He saved Scout's life. I will always be grateful to him for that."

"I hope not too grateful," Jake joked, hiding his true feeling that Stevie might be a threat to his relationship with his new wife. "Oh, really? You could have fooled me. Judging by the number of times I see him in his new truck

drive by, with Stevie practically hanging out the window —
"

Katherine interrupted. "I have no fear of Stevie. He's not a stalker. End of story."

Jake threw up his hands in exasperation. "Okay, case closed. What did he offer?"

Katherine read on, and said with a smile. "Full price."

"What bank is going to give him a mortgage with his criminal record?"

"Jake," Katherine said, looking up with a disapproving look.

"I'm serious. He just started his electrical business. The down payment will be at least twenty percent. Where does he have that kind of money?"

Katherine read the offer again. "It's in cash. All cash at closing."

Jake's eyes widened and he blurted, "Cash? I won't go there." He took the document and read it again, this time more thoroughly. "Katz, it's your house. Are you going to accept it?"

"Let me ask the cats. After all, their favorite room in the mansion faces the Foursquare. But first I've got to let them out of their playroom." Ever since the explosion, whenever she left the house, Katherine locked the cats in the playroom. In light of the mansion's reputation as being a murder house, it was a good idea not to have them running around while she was gone. Normally, she would hire Elsa the cat wrangler to sit with them, but Elsa wasn't available. And today Katherine was only gone for a few hours.

"I know our cats are extraordinary, but how will they let you know if they approve or not?" Jake inquired.

"I'm kidding," she said, amused. "I'm just stalling for time to consider Stevie's offer, that's all."

"Good idea. In the meantime, I'll let them out. I've got to go upstairs anyway and get out of these wet clothes. I need to put on my snow diggin' suit." Once again Jake lapsed into his country accent.

Katherine asked, "Do you ever speak that accent with your colleagues?"

"Hale no, woman. I save that way of talkin' jess fer you."

Katherine giggled. "Okay, get out of here."

"Actually, Mrs. Cokenberger, I'm going outside to do a little more snow shoveling." He reached over and pulled Katherine into a kiss. "I'll need a kiss for the effort."

Katherine smiled, and watched him leave. Then she thought, *Do I really want Stevie Sanders living next door? I think he has feelings for me.*

She picked up her cell and called her best friend, Colleen, who lived in an apartment in the nearby city.

"Hey, Carrot Top, do you have a minute?"

"Sure. What's up?"

"I just got an offer on the yellow Foursquare."

"Shut the door! Really? I thought that would *never* happen. Katz, you don't sound too happy about it. Seller's remorse?"

"I feel guilty about selling a haunted house."

"But you're not. Katrina has crossed over. I'd take the money and run. One less piece of real estate you have to worry about."

"This is true," Katherine agreed. From her great-aunt's estate, she'd inherited several Erie properties, some of them rentals. Although she hired a property manager to handle them, she didn't like being a landlord, especially since one of her buildings had been damaged by an arsonist several months earlier. "So, here's the interesting part. You won't believe who made the offer."

"That friend of Stevie Sanders that looks like a Sasquatch."

"Close, but try Mr. Stevie Sanders. He, himself, and —"

"Are you kidding? Oh, Katz, I didn't see that coming."

"What should I do? I really want to sever my ties with the house."

"Katz, by severing ties with the house, you establish ties with a man who was a crim. What if he doesn't stay clean? What if his crim father moves in?"

"For Stevie's sake, I hope that never happens."

"Exactly. What does Jake think about it?"

"He thinks Stevie is a stalker because he sees him drive by a lot."

"Well, is he?"

Katherine answered reluctantly, "I'm not sure."

"Then don't sell the house to him. There has to be someone else who will buy it."

"Really? Even with Margie's stunning interior rehab, there weren't any takers during the previous listing."

"Katz, why don't you just take it off the market and keep it? Sounds to me you need to think about it some more."

"Yeah, you're right. Listen, I've got to go upstairs and check on the cats."

"Okay, talk to you later," Colleen said, then hurriedly added, "Hey, before I forget, Mum called and said she ran into an old school friend of ours."

"Who?"

"Remember Madison Orson?"

"The model?"

"Uh-huh. Mum said she ran into her on 47th Street. Madison said she was working some place nearby as a temp."

"I didn't think there were any modeling agencies on 47th Street."

"No, not modeling, but a temporary reception job."

"Reception?"

"Yes, that's what she said. I hope you won't get annoyed with Mum, but . . . "

Katherine thought, *What has Mum done now*? She loved Mum like her own mother, but sometimes Mum didn't make smart life choices. In fact, Katherine still hadn't forgiven Mum for disabling the pink mansion's security system to let in a murderer. That foolish mistake nearly cost Jake his life. The aftermath wreaked so much havoc in her life, she had to go through counselling. "But what?" she asked, hesitantly.

"Mum told her about Jake and you getting married. Madison said she wanted to call and congratulate you. Mum gave her your cell number. Hope you don't mind."

"That's okay," Katherine said. "I'd love to talk to Madison. Do some catch-up. It's been years since I've spoken to her."

"Oh, 'tis grand. Mum also gave Madison your address because Madison wants to send you a gift."

"Oh, she doesn't have to do that. Did Mum get Madison's number?"

"Ah, no. She said that Madison had to hurry off because she was late getting back to her job."

"Okay, cool."

Colleen quipped, "Let me know if Stevie Sanders is going to be your new neighbor."

"Will do." Katherine pressed the end call button and walked upstairs to the cats' playroom. When she put the key in the lock, she wondered why the cats were being so quiet on the other side. Normally when they heard her climb the stairs, they'd be waiting at the door, ready to bolt out as soon as she opened it. But today she found the cats snuggled together on the lower perch of the largest cat tree. Scout and Abra's paws hung over the platform.

"Hi, guys and dolls," she said, walking over.

"Mao," Dewey belted, waking up.

"Why are my treasures sleeping as one giant fur ball? You've got other cozies in this room. Are you trying to keep warm?"

"Ma-waugh," Scout confirmed, jumping down. She stretched, then rubbed her face on Katherine's leg.

Katherine gently picked up Scout and held her close. "You've been sleeping a lot, magic cat. Should I be worried about you?"

She surmised that Scout, in the past few months, had too many outside, stressful adventures. Lately, all

Scout wanted to do was sleep. Katherine startled when she heard someone climbing the stairs.

Jake called from the first landing. "Katz, are you up here?"

"I'm in the playroom."

Jake walked into the room, and patted Scout on the head. "I'm sorry. I forgot to let them out."

"You weren't outside very long. Surely, you can't be done shoveling."

Jake laughed. "A young entrepreneur walked by carrying a mighty nice lookin' shovel, so I hired the lad to finish for me. I gave the kid twenty bucks. He acted like it was a million dollars."

Scout began struggling to be put down. "Ouch, Scout. Your back claws are really sharp."

Jake walked down the hall, and started to unlock the attic door. Scout darted down the hall to join him. Jake said to the Siamese, "You better ask your mom."

Katherine walked into the hallway. "I'm sorry, Scout, but cats and bats don't mix. Let's go back into the playroom."

Scout fired off her signature sapphire-blue glare, then hiked her tail and sprinted into the playroom.

"Good girl," Katherine praised.

Standing by the attic door, Jake waited impatiently. "Hurry up," he prodded.

Distracted, Katherine forgot to relock the cat playroom door. "I'm coming as fast as I can," she offered. "Should I wear protective gear?"

"Actually, Sweet Pea, I was up there earlier, investigated every nook and cranny, and didn't see any winged creatures."

"That's encouraging," she said, mounting the stairs after him. On the landing, Jake turned and said, "Boo!"

Katherine grabbed the stair rail. "Don't do that," she said, pressing her other hand to her chest and sneezing. "Jake, first thing we need to do is dust."

The floored attic was a wide-open space, separated by chimneys for the fireplaces on the first floor. The combination furnace-and-air-conditioning unit for the second story stood off to the side, near the east side of the house.

Katherine rarely went into the attic. It was dark from inadequate lighting, stuffy, and dangerous to walk in because of the floor boards that were warped, damaged, or missing. Under her great aunt's will, Orvenia's belongings were donated to the Erie Museum or to charitable organizations. Katherine had diligently sorted through the mounds of "stuff," which reminded her of King Tut's tomb. At the time, she hadn't officially inherited the house or the money yet, but wanted to make sure she sorted fine antiques and valuable personal papers from junk. She hired a crew to remove most of the things, but had kept several empty wardrobe trunks, two antique wood chests, and a tall, antique grandfather clock with a cracked glass door. One of its weights lay on the floor, and seem to cry out, "Fix me."

The grandfather clock had been a thorn in her side. At first the museum wanted it, but later, the now-deceased museum curator, Robbie Brentwood, had declined, stating it needed too much work, especially a new base, because the short, Regency-style legs that held it up were cracked in several places. So, it remained where the movers left it — on a short, knee-height half wall above the first set of attic stairs. Looming like a top-heavy giant, it posed a safety hazard to anyone ascending the stairs.

Jake, who was very enthusiastic about his "new office" project, announced, "I want my desk facing the front of the house." He pointed to the three leaded glass windows in the turret area.

Joining him, Katherine said, "We'll have to put new insulation and drywall up on the walls and ceiling. Also, we'll have to hire an electrician to rewire." She thought of Stevie Sanders, but didn't mention his name.

Jake seemed to read her mind and suggested, "We could hire Stevie Sanders to do the electrical work."

Katherine eyes grew big. She didn't answer, but said instead, "Let's ask Margie to come up with a plan, and have her do the hiring."

Jake walked over and hugged Katherine. "I like your thinkin', Lincoln."

Katherine was enjoying the warmth of Jake's body pressed against hers, because the attic was freezing. They both were startled when they heard a box fall in the far corner of the attic. The sound seemed to come from the vicinity of the furnace.

Katherine jumped. "What was that?"

"I don't know. Let's check it out."

Behind the furnace was a small, closet-sized room. Its walls and ceiling were built of the same pine planks that formed the attic floor. The room's purpose wasn't obvious. Clearly, it wasn't for storage, because there were no shelves or hooks to store or hang things. Katherine was surprised to see the planked door, painted in layers of green paint, partially open.

Katherine had gone into the room one time, and that was enough. It instantly set off bad vibes. She couldn't explain it, and was reluctant to mention her feelings to Jake or Colleen. Jake, being the confirmed skeptic, would offer a rational explanation, while Colleen would want to bring over her spirit-hunting equipment and do a paranormal investigation. Katherine didn't want Colleen dredging up any of the spirits of the poor souls murdered in the mansion, especially Patricia Marston, who was doing just fine in hell, where she belonged.

What was odd about the room was that it didn't have a ceiling light fixture, and because it also didn't have a window, peering into the space was like looking into a dark void. The only way you could see inside was with a flashlight.

"Jake, there's a flashlight hanging on a nail by the front window."

"I'll get it," he said, heading over to fetch it.

Katherine slowly walked to the door, and peered into the space. Four glowing, red eyes met her gaze.

"Raw," Abra cried. "Waugh," Scout added.

Katherine suddenly remembered she'd forgotten to lock the playroom door. "Just great," she said, annoyed.

"How did they get up here?" Jake said, beaming the light toward the cats.

Scout and Abra started swaying back-in-forth in their macabre death dance. They arched their backs, and began bouncing up and down like deranged Halloween cats. Scout hissed; Abra foamed at the mouth. Both cats' eyes were red and reflected an eerie glint in the flashlight's beam.

In a soothing voice, Katherine said to the cats, "It's okay. Come to me," then to Jake, "If you grab Abra, I'll get Scout."

Jake lunged for Abra, and caught the Siamese around the middle. Abra squawked, but didn't try to get down.

Still holding the flashlight, Jake directed the light to Scout who had stopped swaying, but was now slinking toward a missing floorboard.

"Scout, stay. Do not go," Katherine commanded.

It was too late. Scout jumped into the hole; her usually pencil-thin tail bushed out to three times its normal size.

"Jake, hurry and get her," she panicked. "Hand me, Abra. I'll take her downstairs and make sure the other cats don't get up here."

A stampede of rambunctious cats thundered up the attic stairs, and raced to the turret windows, jumping on the sills and looking out. The seal-point kittens, Dewey and Crowie, struggled for position on the middle windowsill, but Lilac and Abby pushed them aside. Iris trotted over to Katherine, and cried a sweet yowl.

Katherine had her hands full. Abra began struggling to be put down, and shrieked in a loud, Siamese voice. "Abra, quit it. You're scratching me."

Jake was on his hands and knees, beaming the light into the hole in the floor. "Katz, I see her. She can't get any farther. There's some kind of wood panel there. Look around and grab anything that will cover this hole. I'm going to reach in for Scout. When I pull her out, we need to cover it before any more of the cats decide to leap down."

"Got it," Katherine said. She moved to the interior of the attic, and found one of her great aunt's trunks — the smaller, lighter weight one, and with one hand, she dragged it over to Jake.

"Okay, that works," he said. "Get ready," he advised. He reached in and seized Scout.

"Waugh," the Siamese sassed. She was covered from head to tail with cobwebs. The cat sneezed, then sneezed again.

Jake hurriedly moved the trunk and placed it on top of the missing floorboard. "That was a close one," he said. "It wouldn't be fun prying up floorboards looking for a very inquisitive cat."

Scout sneezed again. Jake brushed the cobwebs off the cat's fur.

"We've got to get them out of here," Katherine advised. Let's take Scout and Abra down first. Maybe the other cats will follow us."

"That will be the day," Jake said in a disbelieving tone.

"Oh, yeah. You think so. I know the magic word. Treat," Katherine announced, and the other cats raced

67

around her, and fled to their cat room. "Works like magic," she said to Jake who had thrown Scout over his shoulder. Scout blinked an eye kiss.

At the foot of the attic stairs, Jake said, "I thought you closed the door behind you."

"I thought I did, but even if I did close it, Scout can pick any lock. That's why there are three locks on the door. But when the human forgets to engage them, Houdini-cat gets in."

"It'll be different once we remodel the area. Then the cats can come up here anytime. Cokey can make the windowsills in the turret area wider like he did in the kitchen."

Once the cats were safe in their room, Katherine waded through anxious felines to the armoire, where she removed a bag of treats. The noise in the room was deafening as each cat jockeyed to be first. "Inside voices, please," she gently asked.

Once she'd handed out the treats, Jake said in a quiet, agitated voice, "Katz, we need to go back up there."

"Why? I turned the lights out on the way down."

"I think I saw something in the hole."

Katherine's skin began to crawl. "Judging by Scout's and Abra's reaction, whatever is there, can't be good."

"I agree."

Chapter Five

After the amorous mailman left, Madison wondered with disgust. *Why would that creepy man think I'd be interested in him?* She picked up her cell and called her on-and-off boyfriend, Vinny. Vinny answered in a don't-bother-me voice, "Yeah?"

"Why the tone?"

"Mad, can I call ya back. I'm right in the middle of somethin'."

Madison could hear loud laughter and music playing in the background. "Geez, Vinny, are you at the pub?"

"One second. I'm cashing a check." The bartender came over and counted off several one hundred bills, and then left to take care of another customer. "All right, I'm back. How's the love of my life? Still mad about me?"

Madison snickered. "I'm keeping a list of your phony lines. Maybe I can get enough of them to write a book. Listen, are you doin' anything tonight? I know this is short notice, but how would you like to take a trip to paradise?"

"What do you have in mind?" he asked suddenly, with interest.

"I've got a ticket to Chicago. Three glorious nights at a four-star hotel."

"You win the lottery?"

"Nope, I just got a call from my agent. One of the models is sick with the flu, so they need me to take her place. The shoot is Monday morning. Say, how about it?"

"I've gotta work Monday."

"Are you insane? Just call in sick! This is perfect for us. You know how you like those little bottles of booze in the hotel room. Besides, this hotel has a manager's reception. Two free drinks, plus an incredible Italian restaurant nearby."

Vinny laughed cynically. "Incredible Italian restaurant means a chain run by Italian wannabes."

Madison sneered. "I can't talk forever. My boss will see me. Is it a yes or no?"

"Okay. Tell me when and where, and I'll be there, baby."

"I'm making the reservation now. Meet you there after seven. I'll send the itinerary to your phone."

"The things you talk me into," he said. "Ciao."

Madison made the second reservation, then waited until six to leave the front desk. Everyone had left, except her boss, Mr. Zhukov, and the security guard. She buzzed herself onto the showroom floor, and walked to the back locker area to extract her purse, a large party bag stuffed with sparkly pink paper, and her coat.

Mr. Zhukov came up to her side and took his coat off a hanger. "Madison, before you leave, I need to ask you a question. Did you receive a package with a postmark from Australia?" he asked in his thick Russian accent.

Madison looked directly into his eyes, "No, the only package we received was addressed to me. You know I'm a shopaholic," she smiled.

Mr. Zhukov nodded. "Yes, judging by the number of packages you get, you must be."

Madison's face reddened. "Is it okay? I mean I only have items shipped here because if I use my apartment address, I'm afraid they'll be stolen."

"No problem," he said, then asked, "Did you hear from our Down Under friend?"

"Yes, he called a few hours ago."

"Did he say he was sending the shipment by registered mail or FedEx?"

"I'm sure he said FedEx."

"Okay, I'm leaving now. My wife and I have dinner reservations. I'll see you Monday. Enjoy your weekend."

"Yes, definitely," she said dutifully.

"Oh, would you mind waiting around for a few minutes in case the package comes," he said, turning.

"Yes, Sir. But I can't stay past 6:30. I have plans."

Mr. Zhukov put his coat on, buttoned it down the front, and said nervously, "If you do get the package, take it to the security office up the street, and have them store it in their vault. I don't trust the one here. Dimitri will accompany you." He looked at Dimitri and spoke in Russian.

The guard nodded, got up from his chair and said, "*Da. Spokoynoy Nochi*," he called after Mr. Zhukov, who hurried out the door. He walked over to Madison and said in broken English. "You no have to stay. I wait."

"You are a lifesaver," Madison said with a big smile, holding up the party bag. "My best friend is having a party for her seven-year-old. I've got to grab a cab and head downtown."

"Ah, *da. Partiya.* No problem. *Nochi,*" he said.

"Night," Madison answered.

Madison finished putting on her coat and watched as Dimitri ducked into the men's room. She was relieved that he wouldn't see her leave.

Heading to the reception desk, she quickly removed the package from her bottom drawer. She put it in the party bag and slipped out of the store. With a conspiratorial grin, she hailed a cab.

A yellow cab whizzed up. She couldn't believe her good luck.

"Where to?" the driver asked.

"La Guardia Airport. And there's a big tip, if you can get me there as soon as possible."

Chapter Six

Jake led Katherine back to the attic. In one hand, he held a flashlight, in the other he carried a floor lamp. "I swore I saw something lying in there," he said. "It looked like some kind of wood box."

"Scout and Abra were over there. Maybe they batted the box into the hole, and that's what we heard. That's probably why Scout jumped in to check it out."

"Could be."

Holding a long extension cord, Katherine rolled her eyes, "Please, I hope it isn't another box of rare coins. That's just what we need is more money."

Jake handed the flashlight to Katherine and set the floor lamp close to the opening. He took the extension cord and snaked it around to the other side of the small room, plugging the cord into the only outlet on that side of the attic. Returning, he got down on his hands and knees and moved the lightweight trunk aside. With both hands he tugged on the damaged floorboard until the nails gave way. He carefully set the board next to the trunk.

Katherine laid on her stomach and peered into the hole. "I see it," she said excitedly, beaming her light on the box.

Jake reached in and pulled out a battered jewelry box.

Katherine stood up. "Maybe it's the family jewels," she said, wondering why a jewelry box was placed in a hole in the floor. Then she had a terrible premonition. "Don't open it," she warned.

"Why?"

"Because of Scout's and Abra's death dance. They only do that when something bad is going to happen."

"I know, Sweet Pea, but I don't think anything bad is going to happen here."

"Jake, no, please don't open it. Maybe it's Pandora's box. Maybe it's something we don't need to see.

Whoever put it there was hiding it from someone. Let's just put it back."

"Now that doesn't sound like the curious Katz I married. It's not locked. See," he said, handing it to her. The bottom of the box fell open and a set of rusted keys dropped to the floor.

Katherine's jaw dropped. "You didn't."

"I didn't do it intentionally," he said defensively.

Katherine reached down and picked up the keys. "In this old house, with tons of locks, it could take us forever to find out which door they unlock."

"Check the door."

"Which door?"

"The one to this room, silly goose."

Katherine gave Jake a skeptical look. "You call this a door? I've learned enough from Margie that this is called a beadboard panel with enough layers of Kermit the Frog green paint to last a million years. How can there be a lock when there isn't even a door handle?"

"Close the door, panel, whatever. Is there anything on the back of it?"

"Just a painted-shut piece of metal."

"Maybe it's a plate cover to hide a lock." Jake moved over, pulled out his pocket knife and began prying the edge of the brass plate. When finished, he jiggled the plate back and forth until he could pivot the plate aside, revealing an old bolt lock, rusted and dusty with years of disuse.

"Cool," Katherine said, trying one of the keys. "Nope, this one doesn't work."

"Let me see the other one," he said, taking the key from her hand. He inserted it into the lock, gave a hard twist and the lock disengaged. "Takes a little muscle," he teased.

Katherine gave an amused look. "Seriously, what was the purpose of this room?"

Jake scratched his chin. "I think it was a secret room."

"What?"

"Did you ever see that movie *Panic Room*?" Jake asked. He often made references to movies to describe a point.

"No."

"It's about this townhouse in Manhattan that had a secret room for the owner to hide in case of a home invasion."

Katherine laughed. "Surely you jest! This room is built with wood. Anyone with a saw could get in."

"Wait. Maybe it wasn't a room to hide in, but a room to escape from."

"How?"

Jake shone the flashlight back into the hole. He felt underneath the floorboard on the left. "I found a handle." Pushing the handle up, he lifted a section of the floor and set it aside.

"How did you know to do that?"

"My parents and I once lived in a ranch house built in the 1950s. The panel to the crawlspace was like this, only the recessed handle was on top. Whoever built this one, didn't want anyone on the floor to see it."

"Secret, I get that part," Katherine said.

Jake stepped down several feet into the opening.

"Be careful. The floor could be rotten."

Setting his flashlight on the floor above, next to the opening, he crouched down and began pressing the walls.

"What are you doing?"

"Trying to see if there's a hidden catch to open it."

"To what?"

Jake continued pressing the walls until a panel on his right popped open.

"What is it?"

Jake was quiet for a moment, then said, "It's an entrance of some sort. Quick, hand me the flashlight. I'll check it out."

Handing Jake the flashlight, she warned, "Be careful!"

"Katz, come down. It's a landing."

Katherine stepped into the hole. "Landing to what?"

Jake beamed the light on a set of stairs.

"Wow," she said, amazed.

"There's no hand rail. Be careful going down. I'll go down first." At the base of the stairs, Jake stopped.

"Why are you stopping?" Katherine asked, trying to look around him.

"It's a dead end." An unpainted wood wall, from floor to ceiling, stood in the way.

"That didn't get us very far," Katherine complained.

"No, look. There's a lock notched into this wall. It's a door." Jake beamed his flashlight on the ancient lock. "Try that other key and see if it fits."

Katherine inserted the key, turned it to the right, then to the left. The door slid open a few inches.

"It's a pocket door," Jake said, sliding it open. Outside was another landing, only the wood floor was of better quality, and the outside panel was the same oak wainscoting used in other rooms of the mansion.

"I had no idea this was here," Katherine said. "Let's find out where it goes."

"Wait, let me go first," Jake said.

"Aye, aye, captain!" Stepping down the stairs after him, Katherine joined Jake on the landing. "This must be the first floor, but why no door? Is there another hidden pocket door?"

Jake began pressing on the walls. "Yes, but . . ." He slid the panel open to a plastered wall.

"It opens to a wall? Who does that? Why wouldn't the builder cut an opening for the first floor? What's the point of having stairs that lead nowhere?"

"Keep going, there are more stairs," Jake said, sprinting down. "Okay, here's the end . . ." Jake stumbled and fell into a dark space.

"Jake, are you all right?" Katherine screamed, beaming her light into the area.

"Yeah, I'm good. Only my ego has been bruised. Some idiot sawed off the rest of the stairs. Be careful. Don't go any farther. There's stuff down here you don't want to see."

"Like what?"

"Can't say," Jake said, looking at several dead mice skeletons. "We need Cokey to replace these stairs, that is, if we ever want to have a fully operational second stairwell."

"Jake, are you sure you're not hurt? You're six-feet-tall—"

"I landed on both feet. No worries, my love. Throw down your flashlight. I've gotta see if I can get out of here."

Katherine tossed the flashlight down.

Looking around, Jake said, "Katz, there once was a door here — well, there still is — but now it's an opening to something metal." He tried to push it. "Hey, I know where this goes. It's underneath the stairway to the basement. This is that big, old cabinet that holds tools."

"Some secret passageway," Katherine kidded. "You have to move the tool cabinet to get out."

Jake brushed the cobwebs out of his hair. "Probably in the Victorian days, this used to be the servant's stairs to the basement."

"How long are you going to stay down there? I'm chilled to the bone."

Still trying to solve the puzzle of the cut-off stairs, Jake noted, "This would have been a perfect escape for your bootlegging great-uncle. If he ever got busted, he could get out of the house this way."

"Why wouldn't he just run out the back door?"

"If he was upstairs when the cops arrived, he could easily take this stairwell, run downstairs, and flee out the basement —"

"Or through the tunnel to the speakeasy next door. It's possible."

Jake shrugged. "I don't know. It's a mystery."

"Should I have Cokey come over and move the cabinet?"

Jake walked over and threw the flashlight back to Katherine. "I don't think so. I don't lift weights for nothing." With both hands, he grabbed the bottom tread of the cut-off staircase and pulled himself up. "See what I mean?"

"Wow, impressed. Well, I've seen enough of the stairway to nowhere. Let's go back to the attic so we can lock the door to the secret room. Oh, and Jake, when the attic becomes your new office, Scout will figure out that lock in a New York minute, so we better have a locksmith replace it."

The two reached the third floor landing when Jake took Katherine by the arm. "What about the box the key was in? It's pretty cool. Just needs to be cleaned up."

"Add it to your project list," Katherine grinned.

"Sure, I'll do it when I come back from Chicago."

Katherine fell into Jake's arms. "I wish you didn't have to go."

"I'm the guest speaker. I have to go."

"I know, but I want you to drive my Subaru."

"Why? The Jeep's fine."

"Just humor me."

"I'll think about it. Wish you were going."

"We just moved back into the house. I don't want to further stress the cats by leaving them for four days."

"Katz, I understand why you're apprehensive about leaving them with a cat sitter — I mean, Elsa. Maybe in time, Sweet Pea, you'll be able to go away from the house without — "

"Worrying that another explosion will take out the back half of the house," she finished. "It seems like it just happened yesterday."

"Understood. Let me kiss that frown off your face," Jake said tenderly, taking Katherine's face into his hands.

Chapter Seven

On his way to see his daughter, Stevie Sanders stopped in a small, eastern Kentucky town to get gas. His half-brother, Dave, was riding shotgun. Getting out of the truck, Stevie asked, "How much farther is it? It's hard to tell with snow on the ground."

"A few miles. I'll direct ya."

Stevie laughed. "Dave, I have a GPS."

"Ah, your GPS sucks. It got us lost three times."

Stevie threw his hands up. "Yep, you're right."

He got out, filled the truck's tank with gas, then cursed when the machine was out of receipt paper.

He opened the truck door, "Hey, bro, wanna get out and stretch your legs? I've got to go in and get a receipt."

"Who cares? I never get my receipts. When did you get so fussy?"

"Ain't sayin'."

As soon as Stevie cleared the gas station door, the man behind the counter recognized him. "Stevie, is that you? Man, do you look different. Cut your hair?"

"Howdy, Clyde. How's business been in these parts?"

"Not too good with the new interstate opening, but I can't complain."

"I've started an electrical business in Erie, Indiana."

"That's great," then Clyde's voice changed to concern. "I reckon you're here to pay your respects."

Stevie gave a concerned look. "Who died?"

"You ain't heard?"

"No, Erie's a long way from here."

"I'm sorry to be the one to tell ya. Darlene's dead, man. Died of an overdose about three days ago. Funeral was today, but buddy, you missed it."

Stevie didn't wait for Clyde to give him any more bad news or print the receipt. He ran to the truck and jumped in. Firing up the engine, he peeled out of the gas station parking lot.

"What the hell's goin' on?" Dave asked, barely having time to get back in and buckle up.

"Darlene's dead. Overdose."

"Oh, man. That ain't right."

"Funeral was today."

"We had no way of knowin'."

"I'm gittin' Salina. I don't need any lawyer stuff. I'm her father. I'm taking her back to Erie."

"Slow down. You don't want the law around here to pull you over."

Stevie slowed down, looking for backwoods signs. There weren't any road signs to the "holler." If he'd asked for a refresher course direction from Clyde, he knew the man would have explained in terms of local landmarks, like "where the big wreck was in '97," or to "turn at the tree that was hit by lightning."

"Right there," Dave said. "Dammit, if you don't slow down, you're gonna miss it."

"I did slow down," Stevie complained, turning off the highway onto a snow-covered, rutted road.

Dave said, "Turn your brights on."

"Damn, talk about backseat driver."

"Looks like lots of cars have been down this road."

"Yeah, explains the ruts. The funeral was today. Probably folks from all around have come out to pay their respects to Big Mama."

"For your sake, you better hope Big Mama is in a good mood, and bro, whatever you do, don't drink or eat anything that crazy woman offers you. You ain't one of her friends."

"I got it," Stevie said, pulling up behind a pickup bearing Kentucky plates. A man came up to the truck in front, looked inside, then waved the driver on. When he stepped back to Stevie's truck, he said, "Better git out." Two other men, aiming shotguns at Stevie and Dave, followed.

Stevie whispered to Dave. "Stay calm. Let me handle this."

Dave nervously ran his hand through his buzz cut and was quiet.

Stevie slowly got out of the truck and put his hands up. "Ain't packin'." He recognized Darlene's three brothers, every sorry last one of them.

The first brother, sporting a shaved head and large diamond stud in his ear, said, almost apologetically, "We gotta frisk ya."

"Go for it," Stevie said.

When he finished patting Stevie down, the man said, "Ain't you a bit late? Funeral was this mornin'."

"I come to talk to Big Mama. Can you git word to her that I'm here?"

The man ignored the request. "Who's in the truck with ya?"

"Dave, my brother. Don't you recognize him, Mike?"

The man leaned in the truck and said to Dave, "Nothin' funny is goin' happen if you sit here and don't move."

"Got it," Dave answered, and gave Stevie a side glance. He mouthed the words. "Watch your back."

The two other brothers walked to Dave's side of the truck and continued aiming their guns at him. Dave said, "Call off the posse! I'm just gonna sit here and wait for my brother." One of the men spit out a large wad of chewing tobacco and said to the other, "Why don't we kill 'em while we can? One less Sanders in the world."

The other one said, "Ain't right. He's Salina's uncle."

"I reckon so."

Mike led Stevie down a bricked path to the front door of a multi-level log cabin. When he opened the door, Stevie was amazed by the number of mourners sitting around, eating, talking, some were laughing. A small band, sitting on wood stools, strummed guitars and banjoes — five all together. They played "Rocky Top," but changed the lyrics to, "Good ol' Rocky Top, Rocky Top Kentucky," the last word sung as "can-tuck-e."

Mike spoke to a woman sitting by the performers. "Where's Big Mama?"

She pointed to the nearest door, which was closed.

Mike knocked and walked in, leaving Stevie behind. He returned shortly and directed Stevie to come inside.

Big Mama was sitting behind an oak desk, looking like she'd seen better days than this one, when she'd buried her only daughter. Most of the time, Big Mama was a force to be reckoned with, but today she spoke to Stevie in a sad, strained voice.

"Sit down, Stevie. Still good lookin' as ever. Ain't hard to know what Darlene saw in ya."

"Ma'am," Stevie said, taking off his black knit hat. "I'm sorry for your loss. Darlene and I didn't see eye-to-eye, and I can't blame her for runnin' out when I did a stint at the pen, but I always had great respect for you." He thought the words were flowing to fast from his lips, so he slowed down. He truly meant what he said about Darlene, but he was lying about having respect for Big Mama. He hated her. He didn't like to lie, but it was something he had to do to butter up Salina's grandmother.

Big Mama was instrumental in the breakup of his marriage. She never wanted Darlene to leave the holler, let alone marry a "foreigner." To Big Mama, any man from out-of-state was a damned Yankee. To her, Stevie was worse than a damned Yankee; he was a *Hoosier* Yankee. She'd never met a person from Indiana she liked.

Big Mama said, "You look like you could use a drink." She reached into a drawer and pulled out a bottle of Jim Beam. Then she lined up two glasses. Stevie didn't dare refuse, because if he did, that was considered an insult in this part of the woods. He was wary, and wondered if the bottle was poisoned, but relaxed when she cut the neck with a sharp blade she had in her desk. After she'd poured the whiskey and downed the drink, Stevie drank his.

"Ahhh," he said. "Good stuff."

"Finest."

"Ain't as good as yours," Stevie noted.

"I quit cookin' mash years ago. Ain't becomin' of a lady." She tipped her head back and laughed.

Stevie began, "I came to take Salina home."

"I know that," the woman spat loudly.

Stevie was shocked by her sudden mood change, but not too shocked. He'd seen her histrionics many times before.

"What do you have to offer Salina that I can't?" she asked.

"I have my own business now. I've bought a house in a nice neighborhood. I have nice friends who could help Salina grow up into a fine lady."

"I can offer Salina a place in my business. I'll start her out in our weed operation."

Stevie's eyes widened in disbelief. He was about to counter when Salina walked into the room. She was petite for her thirteen years, with long, blond hair, pulled back into a braid. Her blue eyes were brimming with tears.

"Daddy," she said, running over and throwing her arms around Stevie. "I wanna go home. Take me home."

Big Mama seemed stunned. "But Darlin', don't you want to stay here with Big Mama? Go to school here? Be a part of gramma's business?"

Stevie patted Salina on the back of the head. "Hush, baby cake. I've driven all this way to take you home. Go pack up your stuff."

Salina let go and ran from the room.

Stevie faced Big Mama and began slowly. "I respect your offer, but my daughter wants to come with me."

"You hardly know the girl. Hate to say it, Stevie, but you suck as a father."

Stevie looked down at the table, then slowly looked back up. "Can I have your word that we'll be safely escorted out-of-town?"

"Who's stoppin' ya?"

"Your sons at the end of the lane. There doesn't have to be any bloodshed over this. Big Mama, your daughter is dead, but your granddaughter is still very much alive."

Big Mama leaned back in her chair and said, sadly, "No one would harm a hair on that little love's head. But you, Stevie, I'll have eyes on you. If you mess this up, like you did with Darlene, I'll come after you, and it won't be to share a shot of whiskey, neither."

Stevie nodded. "Understood." He rose from his chair and walked through the door to find Salina. Salina was busy putting something in her backpack. It was struggling. It meowed hoarsely.

She whispered, "Quit it. You've got be quiet. Big Mama hates cats, so do this for me." The cat seemed to understand and stopped wriggling inside the backpack.

"Does the critter have a name?"

Salina's eyes lit up. "I named him Wolfy, because he looks like a werewolf."

Stevie wore a "let's get a move on" expression on his face. "Okay, is that your bag?" he asked hurriedly, looking at a handled plastic bag with the Erie Grocery store logo printed on it.

"Yes, and my backpack."

"That's it?" Stevie said, suddenly feeling sad that his daughter had so few belongings.

"Yep. I'll carry Wolfy."

"Let's get out of Dodge by goin' to the Dodge. I'm takin' my favorite gal back to Erie."

"I heard your old truck got blown up."

"Salina, it wasn't old, but brand new. My new truck is a color you'll appreciate."

"Red?" she asked with a grin.

"Cherry red, baby cake."

Chapter Eight

Nikolai Zhukov sat across from his American wife at the Rainbow Restaurant, drinking a vodka martini and checking text messages for the umpteenth time. His slightly annoyed wife noticed something wasn't quite right.

"Niki," she said, concerned. "What *is* wrong with you? You've picked at the appetizer. You've already downed two martinis. This is unlike you. Are you feeling okay?"

He shrugged off the question. "Please, one minute," he said, holding up his index finger. He tapped a number on his cell and tried to call the Australian exporter again. This time his call went through.

He spoke only for a few seconds, then stood up so abruptly, his chair flew backward, hitting another dinner table, and crashing to the floor. Fortunately, no one was sitting at that table. "You did what?" he shouted into the phone. "You sent it to my receptionist?" his voice boomed even louder. He talked for a few seconds more, then disconnected the call. Taking his wife's hand and kissing it, he said in his Russian accent, "Mary, you have dinner. Take a cab home. I need to get to the bottom of something."

"What?" Mary asked, alarmed. "What's going on?"

"Don't ask," he said throwing his hands up with great finality.

"Oh, 'don't ask.' I will ask. Whatever it is, I'm going with you."

Nikolai gave her a sharp look, then snapped his fingers for the nearest server. Finding one, he said, "Put this on my tab. My apologies, but we have a family emergency."

The server said, "I'm sorry, Mr. Zhukov. I hope everything will be okay."

Nikolai didn't answer. He'd already left the restaurant, and jumped into his limo, which was waiting for him. Mary ran behind him, climbing into the back seat without speaking.

The chauffeur turned and asked, "Where to?"

"Take us back to the jewelry store."

The security guard, Dimitri, met the Zhukovs at the front door. Nikolai brushed past him.

"*Preeveeyet*, Mary," Dimitri said hello with a smile.

Mary didn't answer.

Nikolai threw off his heavy coat, "Dimitri, after I left, were there any more deliveries?"

"*Nyet.*"

"Did Madison say where she was going?"

"A party."

"Where?"

The guard shook his head. "*Ya ne znayu.*"

Still stung by her husband's abruptness in the restaurant, Mary said in a clipped voice. "If you need to know where Madison is, maybe she left information on her computer. Let me see if I can find out something."

"Ah, and that is why I love my wife," Nikolai said proudly.

Mary sat down on the reception chair and began striking the keys. Mary wasn't your typical computer user. She worked as a certified network engineer. In a few seconds, she opened Madison's email and began reading subject lines.

"See anything?" Nikolai asked nervously.

"She does a lot of online shopping."

"*Da,* I know this. What else?"

"Did you know she was planning to fly somewhere? Tonight?"

Nikolai's face turned red. Angrily, he asked, in broken English, "Where she go?"

Mary pulled up the flight schedule, then looked at her watch. "She's scheduled to land at the O'Hare Airport in Chicago in —"

Nikolai cut her off. "I need to find her."

Mary asked suspiciously, "I'm not stupid, Niki. Has this woman done something to you?"

Nikolai raised his hand as if he were going to strike her, then put it back behind him. "Check the airline. See if the plane landed."

Mary turned on her chair, and for the first time since she married Nikolai, she was afraid of him. Hammering the keys again, she read the screen. "Her flight was rerouted to Indianapolis."

Nikolai leaned in and stroked his wife on the head. "My darlink, you have done well, but I must take care of bizzness now. You go home. I explain later. No time."

Mary got out of her seat. Nikolai ushered her outside and into the limo. "Take her straight home," he instructed the driver, "then come back for me."

"*Da,*" the driver said, speeding off.

Back inside the jewelry store, Nikolai started searching through Madison's desk.

Dimitri stood guard at the front door.

Nikolai picked up a spiral-bound tablet of phone messages and read through each one of them, from the day Madison started temping for him. Then a slip of paper fell out of the book and landed upright on the desk. He read the name and address: *Katz, 512 Lincoln Street, Erie, Indiana.* He took out his cell and searched Google maps. Reading the result, he said to the security guard, "Ever been to Indiana?"

"Where?" Dimitri asked, still watching the street.

"*Interesno,*" Nikolai said in Russian. Picking up his cell, he punched in the number of Vasily Chernoff, a very close friend of his and the current Russian mafia boss of

Brooklyn. "Vasily will fix this," he said confidently.

Chapter Nine

On Friday at six o'clock, Chief London drove his Erie police cruiser and parked it in front of the pink mansion. The sun had set, and Lincoln Street was very dark. There were no street lights, but Katherine made a point to turn on both the outdoor post lamp and front porch light. She and the cats watched him from the parlor window. Two of the resident cat thieves were particularly interested in the chief's arrival. Abby jumped down from the window valance, her favorite perch that she shared with Lilac and Crowie. Iris slinked around the Eastlake settee, and seemed to exchange a knowing look with Abby.

"I saw that," Katherine said. "Let's not be picking the pocket of the police chief. I guarantee you won't like the food in jail." She rose from her chair and hurried to open the entry door to the front vestibule. She had to open it before the chief pressed the 'dreaded' doorbell. Dewey was terrified of its sharp sound, and if Katherine didn't answer it right away, he'd go flying through the house, destroying whatever was in his wake.

Katherine was too late. The doorbell rang loudly. Not once, but two shrill rings. "Oops, sorry, Dewey. It's okay, little buddy."

"Mao! Mao!" the kitten boomed, as he ran up the stairs, brushing the lamp on the stairwell table. It wobbled on its base, then righted itself.

Katherine opened the door. "Hello, Chief. Come in. Here, let me take your jacket."

He removed his jacket and handed it to Katherine, who took it to the atrium and hung it on an antique Eastlake hall tree.

Returning, Katherine asked, "How have you been?"

"I can't complain," he said, walking in. "The town has been quiet for a while."

Katherine knew there hadn't been much police activity since the arson fiasco and mansion explosion a few months back.

He carried a vinyl shopping bag. "Listen, I've brought my Croc loafers so I don't track snow on your parquet floors."

Katherine laughed. "I see your wife, Connie, has you well-trained."

The chief chuckled and sat down on the Eastlake vestibule chair. He removed his boots and set them on the boot mat. "I didn't see Margie's truck. Is she coming?"

"Yes, she just texted. She's on her way."

Chief London, Margie, and Katherine formed the goodwill committee that met every month to decide what Erie townsperson or nonprofit project was to receive charity, what kind of charity, and when. In a small town, where everyone knew everyone's personal business,

Katherine was amused that no one knew — yet — that she was the benefactor.

After the chief finished putting on his loafers, Katherine said, "Let's sit in the living room." She slid open the closest pocket door, and the two walked in.

"Any particular chair?" the chief asked, eyeing the Victorian furniture.

"Take your pick," she said.

The chief chose the famous winged back chair that held a morbid history: surviving a murder scene and an explosion. It was also the chair where Abby and Iris hid their loot, but Katherine didn't mention that little ditty about Jack and Diane.

Katherine sat down on a Victorian reproduction love seat. Her newer white vinyl sofa set hadn't survived the smoke from the fire, so instead of having it reupholstered, she had it cleaned, then gave it to charity. She decided to stick with the Victorian theme.

Margie arrived and knocked on the door, having learned that the new Siamese in town was terrified of loud noises. She opened the door and walked into the vestibule. "Hey, it's me. Where are you?"

Katherine called from the living room. "We're in here."

Dewey bolted into the room, in a full dead run, leaving cloisonné vases teetering on tabletops. Katherine leaped off the love seat and caught him in a mid-jump. "Young man, please calm down. It's okay."

"Mao!" the Siamese disagreed.

The chief said, "For a little cat, he sure is loud."

Katherine sat down and set Dewey on her lap. Iris leaped up on the arm and yowled. Iris had adopted Dewey, and was showing him the ropes. Katherine hoped that Dewey's training program didn't include theft. "Miss Siam, you can sit here, too," Katherine said, patting the seat next to her.

Iris had other plans. She jumped down and joined Abby on the floor behind the chief's chair.

Margie walked into the room. "Sorry I'm late. I'm working on this house on Owen Street, and I couldn't find my truck keys. I looked all over. Found them in a weird spot. I think one of my workers is playing a trick on me."

"Where were they?" Katherine asked.

"In the sink," Margie laughed. "I probably spaced out and put them there."

"Maybe the house has a poltergeist," the chief kidded. "Wife and I just watched the movie," he added.

"Oh, before I bring the meeting to order," Katherine said, "Jake gave me a huge box of chocolates before he left for Chicago." Katherine reached over and removed the lid from a large, heart-shaped box.

"Yum," Margie said.

"I'll pass," the chief said. "Believe it or not, I'm a rare breed. I don't like chocolate."

114

"I love chocolate, but I'm allergic to walnuts. Before you two arrived, I was reading the ingredients, and unfortunately, written in fine print was the fact they may contain walnuts."

"If that doesn't beat all," the chief said. "I'm bankin' you can't eat any of them."

"Eek, that's unfortunate, Katz," Margie said, pulling a chocolate out of its paper sleeve. "How long is Jake going to be away?"

"He left yesterday. He'll be back on Sunday — "

The chief interrupted, "You know my wife says I don't have a filter, but weather forecasters in Indy said conditions are lining up for another storm like the one that hit central Indiana in 1978."

"Knock on wood. I don't want to have to go through that again," Margie commented.

"Sounds ominous," Katherine said. "I've been through bad winter storms in New York and Indiana."

The chief continued, "I was twelve when the blizzard of '78 happened. We got hit with a hellava load of snow and record low temperatures. Wind chills were sixty below zero. My parents and my four brothers lived down on Owen Street, close to where you've been workin', Margie. Our power went out, but we were lucky to have a wood-burning fireplace. I remember my brothers and I huddled underneath a blanket, eating animal cookies."

"Animal cookies?" Katherine repeated.

"My mother was well-organized and had the pantry stocked with soups and canned meats, but what kid wants to eat that stuff?"

"You're lucky you had a fireplace. The gas fireplaces in the mansion have electric starters. If the power goes out, that wouldn't do Jake and me any good."

"Many folks throughout the state weren't so lucky. The storm went on for three days. At the end, Indiana got up to forty inches of snow. Do you know what that's like?"

the chief asked, not waiting for anyone to answer, then continuing, "The weight of the snow collapsed roofs, trapped folks in their homes. I'm sorry to say, but there were many casualties of folks freezing to death."

Katherine forehead furrowed with worry lines. "Now I'm *really* worried. I tried to talk Jake out of going."

"Typical Cokenberger," Margie tried to comfort. "Stubborn as a herd of donkeys."

The chief eyed Margie curiously. "Herd of donkeys? That's a good one. Katz, I wouldn't worry. The storm could fizzle out or miss us entirely."

"On that doom-and-gloom note, let's bring this meeting to order," Katherine said, trying to regain her happy disposition. "Chief, it's your turn to hit me with your best shot. Who in Erie needs help?"

"I don't know if you've heard it or not, but someone you know very well has met on hard times."

Margie nodded. Katherine wondered what the chief was going to say next, and how Margie seemed to know already.

"Who?"

"Stevie Sanders."

"What? I thought things were going well for him. He's back on the job because I see his truck go by."

"Then you haven't heard?" the chief asked solemnly.

"Heard what?" Katherine leaned forward in her chair.

"His ex-wife overdosed on meth. Folks at the diner said Stevie drove down to Kentucky to find her, and found out the bad news."

Margie said, "Katz, her name was Darlene. She's been messed up for years, and even did a stint in jail."

The chief added, "Petty thief, shoplifting, possession, to name a few. She's got quite a rap sheet for a small town."

"I didn't know Stevie had ever been married. Personally, I don't think of Stevie as the marrying kind," Katherine noted as an afterthought.

Margie added, "Yep, he's got a reputation as a regular 'love 'em and leave 'em' type of guy."

The chief said in a matter-of-fact voice, "So, my candidate this month is Stevie."

Katherine looked amazed. "Really? He drives a brand new truck. It seems there are other people in Erie who need more help than Stevie."

"Not that I'm a fan of the Sanders," Margie began, "but I think Stevie's trying to get his life back on the right track. And then again, kiddo, he'll need furniture for that big old house next door."

Katherine asked amused. "How did you know he bought the house? I just accepted the offer."

"Little birdie told me," Margie said sheepishly.

"One named Lucy — the realtor?"

"Ain't sayin'."

The chief scratched his beard, which he kept stylishly short. "Not sure how he came up with the money for a house. That's none of my business unless he got it illegally. I have no way of knowing."

Margie interjected. "I know the answer to that, Chief."

Katherine eyebrows rose in wonderment of Margie's ability to find out information.

"His mother died several years ago and left him money."

"If he's inherited money, I don't understand why I should give him more money when there are so many other people in Erie that need help."

Margie answered, "Lucy said Stevie spent the entire inheritance to buy the Foursquare."

"But why would he do that? My mom used to say never put all of your eggs in one basket."

The chief said, "It all makes sense to me. He wants to lead a respectable life. What better way than to buy a house in a nice neighborhood."

"Where does Stevie live now?" Katherine asked, picking up Dewey and kissing him on the head. Dewey struggled to get down, jumped off her lap, and trotted into the atrium.

"I know the answer to that," Margie said. "Bill, one of my drywall guys, said he lives with a friend down by the tracks."

"Surely not. I've driven down there. It's a mecca of dilapidated mobile homes."

"You mean trailers. Folks around these parts call them trailers," the chief offered.

"Wow, if I'd only known," Katherine said. "I've already paid off his hospital bill. Oops, I didn't mean to divulge that. This is strictly private and confidential. I don't want folks down at the diner to know this."

Margie answered, a little offended, "Of course, nothing that is said in this room leaves this room."

The chief nodded.

Katherine continued. "I owe a lot to Stevie. He saved my life, and Scout's."

"Waugh," Scout agreed from the middle turret window, sitting on the windowsill and watching snow fall.

The chief gave Katherine a concerned look. "Katz, the Sanders are an untrustworthy and treacherous bunch. I'm not completely convinced that Stevie will stay in the good graces of the law. I'd watch your back, if I were you."

"I'll take that under advisement," she answered, then, "I'll have fun with this charity. I love shopping for furniture."

Looking around the well-appointed period room, the chief said, "Well, kindly suggestion, I don't think Stevie is the type for fancy Victorian furniture because it looks nice, but plays hell on your back."

Katherine smiled. "Okay, I'll buy some manly furniture."

Margie suggested. "I know a furniture store that sells mission-style. There's a recliner that I bought for Cokey and he loves it."

"Does the furniture store have a web address? I like to do things online."

"Sure, I'll email it to you."

The chief started to get up, then sat back down. He let out a loud laugh. "Look at that little varmint." He was gazing across the room at Iris, who clutched a silver pendant in her V-shaped jaw. She was straddling the chain like a giant spider.

"Iris, what do you have?" Katherine asked, getting up and investigating the scene. "Drop it! Oh, good heavens. It's my wedding necklace. The one Mum gave me."

Margie leaped out of her chair. "What? No way."

"If I recall," the chief began. "It's the one you lost last September."

"When I was kidnapped! Where did you find it?"

"Wasn't me who found it. The caretaker of the old asylum found it in the shack next door. It was stuck between two floorboards. He said it was the darndest thing because he'd been in and out of that room a dozen times, even polished the floor, and didn't see it. But one day the sun was coming through the window, and the silver in the necklace beamed up like a light ray."

Iris didn't want to let go of her prize and continued clutching it in her jaw. "Let go," Katherine pleaded. Iris clenched her jaw even tighter.

Abby found her opportunity and fished the chief's cell out of his pocket. She was half-way off the chair with it clutched in her jaw when Katherine saw her. "Abby, give it back." The chief turned in his seat to stare into the eyes of the ruddy-colored thief. Abby lowered her head, dropped the phone and cried demurely, "Chirp." Then with one hard whack of her paw, she batted it to the floor.

Finally, Iris let go of the necklace, and yowled sweetly. "Thank you, Miss Siam," Katherine said affectionately. "Chief, was the necklace in your pocket, your jacket pocket, or in that bag you brought in?"

He retrieved his cell and laughed. "I brought it in the shopping bag. Your cats are pretty darn smart, but speaking as a lawman, I suggest you never take them into a store."

Katherine giggled. "After Lilac destroyed the cakes at the bake sale, I doubt I'll ever take my cats to another public place. Thank you so much for returning it. I thought I'd never see it again."

The chief looked at his watch. "Gotta get goin'."

"Me, too," Margie seconded, "but first I want another chocolate."

"Have two or three," Katherine suggested.

Margie hung around until the chief left. "Listen kiddo, when you're buying furniture, order a bedroom set for a young girl about thirteen-years-old."

"Why?" Katherine asked, wondering what else Margie knew about Stevie Sanders.

"He has a daughter. I didn't want to say it in front of the chief because he probably thinks I'm a busybody, but with Darlene dead, Stevie will have custody. In fact, I heard he didn't go to Kentucky to check on his ex-wife. He drove down to get his daughter."

"Wow. I didn't have a clue. Why hasn't anyone told me before?"

"Mayhaps, it never came up in conversation?"

Katherine didn't answer, but thought, *Why hasn't Jake told me about it? Did he know?* Then shifted the subject, "I wouldn't have a clue what to buy a girl of thirteen. Can you do me a favor?"

"Sure," Margie said, popping another chocolate in her mouth.

"Can you go to the furniture website and get Shelly's opinion? She's close in age to Stevie's daughter. Maybe Shelly can come up with something a teen would like."

"Gotcha," Margie said, walking out the door.

"See ya," Katherine said, borrowing one of the sayings Jake used.

                    *   *   *

After the committee disbanded and Margie left,

Katherine walked into the kitchen to make a cup of tea. As

she filled the kettle, the doorbell blared its angry alarm.

"One of them must have forgotten something," she

surmised out loud. "Dewey," she called. "It's okay."

The kitten was en route to the kitchen, did a dead

stop, and then sprung for Katherine's desk. Landing on the

keyboard, he quickly caught his balance and sprung off,

leaving the keyboard dangling precariously over the edge.

Katherine righted the keyboard and mouse, then

was curious about what was displayed on the computer

screen: a sparkling diamond glistened on the display. *I*

know Jake couldn't have surfed this up, she thought. *I've*

got enough jewelry from Jake to last me a lifetime. But why

would the cats?

The doorbell sounded again.

"All right, already," she called, annoyed. Walking through the living room, she discovered Dewey had catapulted off the coffee table and knocked down the box of chocolates. Various-sized confections were strewn across the floor. Katherine knew chocolate wasn't good for cats, so she closed the pocket door behind her. She'd clean up the mess later.

"I'll be right there," she said loudly to the front door, in an effort to make the person outside stop ringing the bell. Rushing to answer, she stopped to peek out the sidelight. She didn't recognize the woman, who wore a full-length mink coat. Wisps of blond hair stuck out from her matching fur hat. She rang again.

"May I help you?" Katherine said through the glassed sidelight.

"Katz, is that you? It's me, Madison. Let me in. I'm turning blue."

Katherine hurriedly opened the door. "Madison?" she said in a surprised voice. "What on earth are you doing here? Come in, before you freeze to death."

The two childhood friends hugged, then Katherine asked, "Is that your car?"

"Yes, why? Did you think Santa and his reindeers brought me here?" she quipped.

Katherine was still in shock. "You drove by yourself from Manhattan to Indiana in this storm?"

"No, Dummy, I drove it from Indianapolis. I'm on my way to Chicago."

For a moment Katherine was caught off-guard, then she remembered her old friend called her "Dummy," while Katherine called her friend "Rummy."

"Okay, Rummy."

The seven cats stood at a distance, oddly standing in a row like soldiers, looking at the woman with feline curiosity. They eyed the coat and hat even more. Abra licked her lips. "Raw."

"Oh," Madison jumped back, suddenly very agitated. "What are those?"

"My cats. What's wrong?"

"No, the two in front. They don't look like any cats I've ever seen."

"Madison, they're my Siamese. Scout and Abra."

"Dummy, I can't come in until you . . . you . . . ," she stuttered. "Put them up."

"They won't hurt you," Katherine reassured. "They're just being curious, but if you want me to, I'll take them upstairs." Before she had time to herd cats, Scout cried a loud "waugh," and most of the other cats followed her up the stairs. Iris hid behind the Eastlake hall tree, while Abby tried to blend in next to the oak table nearby. Katherine was too distracted to notice them.

"I must apologize, Katz. Colleen's mom told me you had cats, but I didn't know you had . . . so many."

"Come in the parlor and sit down."

Still standing in the same spot, Madison said, "La-di-da. A 'parlor,' she says."

"It's in here," Katherine directed. "Do you want something to eat or drink? I can fix you something."

"No, I'd rather sit for a while." Sitting down close to the window, Madison said, "The cats gave me a scare, especially those two tall, skinny ones. I must be going crazy, but I swear their eyes were red."

"Sometimes if the lighting is just right, Siamese eyes will appear to be red, but trust me, there isn't anything scary about them. They're the sweetest cats. Let me take your coat."

"No, I'll hold on to it for a while. I'm chilled to the bone." She placed her Chanel tote bag on her lap and began rummaging through it, then put the bag on the floor next to her chair.

"I better go upstairs and shut the cat's playroom or else they'll come back down here. I know you're not a cat person, but cats instinctively gravitate to the person who either doesn't like cats, or is afraid of them. It's their nature."

"Whatever," Madison said dismissively.

Katherine left the room and thought how strange it was that a friend she hadn't seen since high school graduation was now in Indiana, sitting in her parlor. Before shutting the cats' door, she did a head count. Two were missing.

"Oh, great," she lamented. "I hope they're not in the room freaking out Madison." Hurrying back downstairs, she found her friend madly texting someone. Katherine waited until she was finished, then said, "You look great. We need to do a major catch-up. Are you still modeling?"

"I was, but I'm twenty-eight now, and there are younger models out there taking the jobs. That's one of the reasons why I'm headed for Chicago. I have a gig there, and then I'm flying back to NYC."

"Colleen said that you were temping."

"Yes, believe it or not," Madison laughed. "Can you imagine? I regret not going to business school after I graduated. I wish I had better computer skills. I've been doing reception jobs."

"Really?" Katherine asked. "In Brooklyn or Manhattan?"

"Mid-town Manhattan. Sometimes the job lasts six weeks, if I'm lucky, or a few days. Lately, I've been working on 47th Street."

"That's not far from where I used to work on Fifth Avenue."

"Cool, but I don't want to bore you with me. Colleen's mom said you inherited big bucks, and a mansion. Plus, you married a hunk."

"Are you married? Engaged? Dating?" Katherine inquired in an effort to divert the mention of inheritance.

"None of the above. Single and free, that's me."

"So, if your modeling job is in Chicago, how did you end up at my door in a snow storm?"

Madison shifted nervously in her seat, then began. "Because of this wretched weather, my plane was rerouted to Indianapolis. I didn't have a clue when the next flight would be. You know me. I hate to wait, so I rented that piece of junk out there, and drove. Thank God for GPS or I'd never have found this place."

"You brought your GPS," Katherine asked in want of something better to say.

"No, Dummy, it's built into the car."

"Yes, I know, I have one in my new Subaru," Katherine said, not liking being called *dummy* as an adult. It was funny at age ten, but not so much now.

"A Subaru? Why aren't you driving a Mercedes or a Bentley?"

Katherine answered with an observation, in an attempt to once again steer the conversation away from material things. "Your blond hair looks nice with your blue eyes."

Madison laughed. "I've been a blonde for years."

"I'm trying to remember the last time I saw you. Was it our high school —"

"Graduation," Madison finished. "Remember when I walked up to get my diploma, and my sleeve caught on the hand rail. I tripped going up the steps and fell into the arms of the principal."

Katherine laughed at the memory. "That's not as bad as me tripping down the steps."

Madison looked at her watch. "How far is Chicago from here?"

"It's about a two-hour drive, but in this weather, it will take you longer. Jake is in Chicago this weekend. He drove up yesterday."

"Who's Jake? Is that your husband?"

"Yes, Jake Cokenberger."

Madison brought her hand up to stifle a laugh. "Coke and burger. Hee hee! That's funny," she said sarcastically.

"Cokenberger," Katherine said, enunciating each syllable. She was taken aback by her old friend's abruptness.

"What's he doing in Chicago?" Madison asked.

"He's delivering a paper — "

"You married a truck driver? I guess it doesn't really matter these days. When you're a millionaire you can marry just about anybody."

"Jake doesn't deliver papers. He's a history professor." Normally, Katherine would have gone into more detail about what Jake did for a living because she was very proud of him, but Madison's condescending manner put her off. She cautiously continued. "Besides, Madison, what's wrong with being a truck driver? They help put food on the table."

"Is he a redneck?" Madison asked, getting up and walking over to the parlor window. She moved the lace panel and looked out. "Dumb as a rock, but good in bed?"

Katherine's face reddened. "Madison, really? My husband is *not* a redneck. People in this part of the globe do not take kindly to being called a redneck."

"Oh, don't get all fired up. That's something I specifically remember about you. You overreact at *everything!*" She said the last word with exaggerated emphasis.

Katherine struggled not to reach over and pinch her friend, like she used to when they were in elementary school. Back in the day, when they wore matching plaid skirts with crisp white blouses, their moms ironed laboriously. Calming herself, she broached another topic. "I'm surprised you wear fur."

"Why?" Madison asked defensively.

"Because I distinctly remember you didn't approve of people who did."

"That's when I was poor. Now it's a different story."

"You were never poor."

"Yes, I was. Have you forgotten? You came from a poor home, too."

"No, I didn't. My parents did okay."

"Well, whatever," Madison said with a wave of her well-manicured hand. "Judging from what Colleen's mom said, you're living the life of Riley."

Katherine became quiet, and wondered how she could get rid of this woman who seemed to have been invaded by a body snatcher. She couldn't believe this was her sweet little friend from next door, who spent hours at her house, cutting out paper dolls, or just sitting on the townhouse stoop watching people walk by. *I wonder what happened in Madison's life to make her so cynical,* Katherine wondered.

Still looking out the window, Madison asked, "Who do you know that drives a pickup truck?"

"In this town, practically everyone drives one."

"Ooh, la la! A tall, handsome man just got out. Katz, he's walking up the front walk."

Katherine rose from her chair, and wondered who it was. She moved to open the door before the man sounded the dreaded doorbell. "Stevie?" she asked, surprised.

"Ma'am," Stevie said, brushing the snow off his knit hat. "Is Jake around? I'd like to have a word with the two of you."

"Please, come in. How are you? How's your hand?" Last September, Stevie, trying to save her life and Scout's, took a bullet in the palm of his left hand; another bullet hit his right shoulder.

"Hand is good. How have you been, good lookin'?"

Katherine stepped back a few feet for a better comfort zone. Stevie's compliments always made her uncomfortable. "Jake's in Chicago."

Stevie caught Katherine's eyes. "Not proper for me to come inside, when the mister ain't home. What would those liars down at the diner make of it?" Stevie turned and started to open the door.

"Stevie, I'm not alone. An old friend is here. Would you like to come in for a minute? I have a warm fire blazing in the parlor."

"And where's that? You gotta remember, I ain't never been inside your house before."

"'*Haven't* been,' Stevie," Katherine corrected. "I hope you don't mind, but I'm making it my New Year's resolution to help you improve your grammar, one word at a time."

Stevie smiled. "Haven't," he said, winking.

"I can hang up your jacket."

"No need." Stevie took off his jacket and draped it over the back of the Eastlake chair by the boot mat. Underneath, he wore a short-sleeved black T-shirt. He stomped his boots on the rug, but didn't offer to remove them.

"This way," Katherine directed.

Madison had taken her seat, and eyed the newcomer with sultry eyes. She did a quick up-and-down sweep of Stevie, and said, "Katz, who's this blond, handsome specimen of a man?"

Stevie gave her a cold, hard look.

"This is my friend, Stevie Sanders. Stevie saved my life a few months back."

"I can't think of anyone else who I'd much rather save mine," she said, then added to Stevie, "Excuse me for saying, but have you ever thought about modeling? I have connections in Manhattan."

"No, Ma'am."

"Stevie, this is Madison," Katherine finally introduced. "She's a model in New York City."

Madison continued her appraisal of Stevie. "You've got the bluest eyes I've ever seen."

Stevie answered evasively, "Ma'am, there's somethin' you need to know about me. I like my cars fast, and my women not to go over the speed limit."

Madison threw her head back and laughed. "Hee hee! I love a man with a sense of humor."

Annoyed, Stevie said to Katherine, "Is there someplace where I can talk to you — alone?"

"Sure," Katherine said, "Follow me to the living room. I'll be back in a minute, Madison."

"Okay, Dummy."

Katherine frowned. She slid open the pocket door. "Stevie, you can sit anywhere."

"I'm okay. I've been ridin' in the truck for hours. It'll do me good to stand." Observing the chocolates on the floor, Stevie kidded, "Have a fight with your valentine?"

Katherine rolled her eyes. "No, but my cat did."

Madison called after them, "Don't leave on my account. Oh, I love the tattoos on your arms. Before you leave, I'd like to see them close-up."

Katherine said under her breath, "What *is* wrong with her?" No sooner had she said that when someone barged through the front door without knocking or ringing the doorbell. A man's voice began shouting at Madison, who was now standing in the atrium, hanging up her fur coat.

Stevie raised his hand in a 'stop' gesture. He shook his head, then walked over to Katherine. He gently took her by the arm. He pushed her back into the far living room corner, as if to shield her from the two people on the other side of the door.

Madison barked, "I told you to wait in the car. I was just about to ask her, when you rush in here like a bull in a china shop."

The man said firmly. "We can't stay here tonight. We need to go. Now! I think they've found us."

"No way. How?"

"How?" he asked in amazement. "What's-a-matta-with-you? You told me you freakin' bought our airline tickets with your boss's credit card; you made the reservations from your company's email. What idiot does that from where they work? Why didn't you just print them a freakin' itinerary?"

"Whatever," she dismissed. "You're overreacting. Our flight was rerouted, and we drove here. How would they *know* about this place?"

"No time for your bullcrap."

"Fine, I'll get my purse." She stomped into the parlor, and panicked. "Oh, no! No! No! Where's my purse?"

"Calm down. Where'd you put it?"

"Right by my chair," she pointed.

"Well, it's not there now. Did it sprout legs and walk somewhere?" he asked, looking around. "There it is, by that ugly coat rack."

Madison rushed over, stooped down, and picked up her tote bag. A startled Siamese flew out from behind the Eastlake hall tree and ran full-speed up the stairs. "That damn mangy cat must have dragged it over here."

"Hurry up!" he demanded.

"Give me time to put on my coat," she said, pulling her coat off the hall tree's hook. "I've got to tell Katz I'm leaving."

"There isn't time. I'll meet you at the car." The man left, impatiently slamming the door behind him.

Katherine tried to walk past Stevie, but he held her fast. "Stevie, let go of me. I want to get Madison out of my house."

The front door slammed again.

Stevie released his grip. "I'm sorry, Ma'am."

147

Katherine ran to the sidelight and gently lifted a corner of the lace curtain. A four-door black sedan, with the passenger side window down, pulled up to the sidewalk. Inside the vehicle, a man began firing an automatic pistol; it riddled the rental car with a barrage of bullets. When the shooter saw the man running down the sidewalk, he shot him several times.

Madison hid behind one of the porch wicker chairs, and didn't move until the vehicle sped off. The wounded man staggered and collapsed by the car, in the drainage ditch at the edge of the street.

Katherine tried to open the door, but Stevie stopped her. "They ain't done yet. Call 911."

Madison hurtled off the porch, slid on a patch of ice, righted herself, and skidded past the motionless man. She didn't stop to check on him, to see if he were dead or alive. Instead, she headed for the driver's side of the Dodge Ram truck.

"Stevie, she's trying to get into your truck," Katherine said in a frightened voice.

"No, freakin' way. My daughter's in there."

Chapter Ten

Jake retrieved his Jeep Wrangler from a Chicago underground parking garage and drove to the entrance of a four star hotel. His friend from the university, Professor Wayne Watson, paced out front, rubbing his hands together in both anxiety, and an effort to keep warm.

Several years earlier, Wayne used his metal detector to find a stash of gold coins worth millions, buried near the grave of Amanda Colfax — daughter of Katherine's great-uncle William. Wayne was tall and a dead ringer for Buddy Holly, complete with thick, black-framed glasses. The only difference was the glasses were broken in the middle, and Wayne, being a frugal soul, had taped them with electrical tape.

Jake stopped and put the Jeep in neutral.

Wayne climbed in, clutching his laptop, which he placed on the floorboard.

"Where's your luggage?" Jake asked.

"I left it with Charlie." Charlie was another professor from the university attending the same conference.

"Okay, let's go. I've gotta warn ya, it's gonna be a bumpy ride. The weather reports aren't good. We could get the storm of the century, but not to worry, my friend. My ol' Jeep and I have been there, done that," Jake laughed unconvincingly.

Wayne caught the apprehension in Jake's voice. "I'm *so* grateful you are taking me back early. Leslie went into labor two hours ago, and I promised I'd be there for our first baby." Before Jake and Katherine got married, Wayne had married his girlfriend, Leslie. Leslie was an administrative assistant for the university vice president and had been one of Katherine's first students in her computer training course.

Jake eased out of the hotel's circular drive onto an empty side street. He glanced around and observed,

"Hardly any cars on the road. It looks like we've got the highway to ourselves."

"Yeah, fewer cars to slide into us and force us off the road."

"Streets aren't bad. The city has been keeping them clear. I'm just worried about US 41."

"Driving here, well, actually riding here — Charlie drove his Land Cruiser — it looked like the state plows were keeping up with the snow."

"Wait until we get around Kentland, then we'll see how the plows are doing."

"The land is flat as a pancake, and when the wind kicks up, those windmills will be a flyin'."

Jake pulled onto Lake Shore Drive. "Wayne, can you do me a favor? Can you text Katz and let her know we're on our way?"

"Sure," Wayne said, retrieving his cell phone from his second shirt pocket. The other one held his assortment of pens and a Hewlett Packard calculator, which he never left home without. "What do you want me to say?"

"Tell her that we left the hotel, that we're coming home, and that I should be in Erie by — "

"Let's factor in your taking me to the hospital. That adds another two hours round trip."

"So, tell her I'll be home around ten."

"Excuse me for asking, but what happened to your cell phone?"

Jake belted out a loud laugh. "One of our cats decided to play hockey with it. Since I've been in Chicago, I've been talking to Katz on the landline in my hotel room."

"Hockey? That's a first."

"Probably Abra. The first time I saw her was at a magician's show, here in Chicago. She fetched a cell phone from someone in the audience. It was a funny ab lib, but the magician didn't think so. That's how Katz and I ended up with her."

"I'm glad you did. You two are the best fur parents around," Wayne laughed. "That what's Leslie calls you — fur parents."

Jake chuckled, then became serious. "Last time I called Katz was last night around six. She said she was sitting by the fire with the cats. She said it was so peaceful watching the snow fall."

"I can imagine a Norman Rockwell scene. Are you glad you're back in the pink house?"

"Yes, I've got plans for a new office in the attic. It's so cold in the house though. I've got to consult with an HVAC expert to see if we can improve the heat. Katz is always complaining about being cold."

Wayne sent the text. A not delivered message popped up on the screen. "For real? We're in Chicago, for crying out loud. There should be great reception here."

"You sure you punched in the right number?"

"Yeah, I hit it from my contacts list. Let me try again." Wayne resent the message. The message returned undelivered. "Sorry."

"Oh, she's asleep now anyway. If I know Katz, she has her cell close by. I don't want to wake her. I'll just try and call her when we get closer to Erie."

With three xylophone notes, the weather app on Wayne's phone displayed a weather advisory message. "Bad news, my friend. We're expected to get a foot of snow — maybe more."

"Then forget US 41, and let's take the interstate, instead. Can you Google us a map on how to get there from here?"

"I'm working on it now."

Chapter Eleven

Stevie stormed out the doorway of the pink mansion and yelled, "Git away from my truck."

"Kiss off," Madison said. She dashed to her rented car, jumped in, fired up the engine, and stepped on the accelerator. The car peeled out, doing a donut skid in front of the mansion. Madison moved the steering wheel like a professional driver, and took off toward US 41.

"Oh, my god. What just happened here?" Katherine shouted after Stevie, terrified. Her first instinct was to run upstairs to check on the cats. They were surprisingly quiet. She panicked. *What if a stray bullet hit one of them, sitting in the window?*

Katherine's mind shifted into auto pilot. She had to check the injured man to see if she could help him. She ran outside, slid on the bottom step, and nearly fell on top of him. When she saw the gaping wound in the man's forehead, she screamed.

Stevie said in a strained voice, "Ma'am, he's dead. Go back in the house!"

In shock, Katherine ignored Stevie's warning. She frantically removed her cell from her jean's pocket. She didn't waste time calling 911; she called Chief London instead. "We've had a drive-by shooting in front of my house. A man is dead — I don't know who he is — he's lying in my front drainage ditch."

"Katz, find a safe place to hide and stay there until we get there," the chief answered.

She turned to run back inside the house, but stopped to look up at the second story window at the room where the cats were. Five very agitated felines sat on the windowsill staring at her; she could hear them wailing. *Finally, they found their voice*, she thought. *But where are Iris and Abby? I've got to look for them.*

Stevie tried to get into his truck but the door was locked. "Salina, open the door." His voice had changed to alarm.

Hurriedly, he fished the truck keys out of his tattered jeans pocket and opened it. "Salina, are you okay?" Stevie's daughter was hunkered down on the floorboard. He reached in and pulled her up.

"Daddy, my backpack."

Still holding Salina against him with one arm, Stevie leaned in so she could pick up her backpack. Salina clasped it against her. She became very upset and started crying. "Wolfy's not moving. I think they shot him."

"It's okay, baby cake," Stevie tried to console. "We'll check on ol' Wolfy when we get inside."

Katherine had returned to the house, and stood at the opened door. Pointing at the living room, she said in a scared voice. "Go in there and lay her down on the sofa."

Stevie walked by. "Lock the door. Cut the lights. Whoever did this is bound to come back."

Katherine turned out the front porch light, then walked through the first floor, turning off more lights. When she returned to the living room, Stevie had placed his daughter on the sofa. Katherine switched on a small cloisonné lamp, then grabbed a fleece throw from the sofa's back and covered her.

"Wolfy's dead," Salina shrieked. "They shot him. I know it, 'cause I can't feel him. He's not moving."

Stevie opened the flap of the backpack. The cat inside howled loudly, then hissed. A long-haired, skinny gray cat with brilliant green eyes spilled out, looked about frantically, then darted behind the marble-top Rococo cabinet.

"Calm down, Salina. Wolfy's okay, but are you? Did you get shot?"

"No, I ducked down when I saw them pull up."

"Who was it? Was it anyone you've seen before in town?"

"Yes!" she shrieked again, then cried even more hysterically.

Stevie held her close and asked with growing concern. "Did the driver see you?"

She nodded. "I think so."

"Tell me about the vehicle. Was it a truck or car?"

"A car . . . a big shiny, black one."

"Could you see who was in it? Two people or one?"

"Two. When you went into the house," she sobbed. "I got bored so I scooched over to your side of the truck and was looking out the side mirror. That's when I saw them. They were coming up fast. I thought they were going to slide into the truck, so I ducked down and braced myself for the crash. When I heard the gunshots, I got down on the floor, and stayed there until you came and got me."

"Salina, did you recognize anyone in the vehicle? Tell me."

Salina sobbed more. "I can't tell you. You'll get mad."

"I won't get mad at anything you tell me. You're my baby girl. Stop crying, and just tell me. When the police get here, they'll need to know."

She mumbled a name.

"I didn't hear that. What did you say?"

"He looked like Grandad."

In a split second, Stevie face changed from shock to anger. He turned to Katherine and asked, "Can I leave Salina with you for a while?"

"Why?" Katherine asked with growing concern. She didn't like the expression on Stevie's face. He was angry. Too angry.

"I need to take care of somethin' right *now*."

"Stevie, the police will be here any second. You're a witness."

"I didn't see a damn thing."

"Daddy, will you come back?" Salina asked warily.

Stevie leaned down and kissed Salina on the top of her head. "Of course. You're my favorite gal. I'll be back as soon as I can. Katz is a good friend of mine. She'll take good care of you."

Stevie yanked his jacket off the Eastlake chair and stormed out of the house. "Lock the door," he yelled, without looking back. He got in his truck, put it in gear, drove down the long driveway beside the mansion, then turned into the back alley.

Salina sat up and cautiously looked at Katherine. "Are you my Dad's girlfriend?"

Katherine startled. "Ah, no, I know your father because a few months ago he saved my cat and my life."

"Yes, my mama told me about it. That's when he got shot," the girl said, then started to cry again. "My mama died."

"I'm so sorry, Salina."

Stevie's daughter looked skeptical. Katherine caught the emotion and changed the subject. "Your cat is behind that cabinet over there. Can you try and coax her out, so we can put her in a cat carrier?"

"Okay," Salina said, more confident that she wouldn't be harmed by this adult she'd never met before. She'd learned at an early age to stay clear of grown-ups, especially those that came to her house, bringing her mother drugs. "But, Ma'am, Wolfy is a boy."

Katherine smiled. "Okay, I'll remember that. Now, I have two cats I need to find. I'm going upstairs for just a minute. Can you stay here?"

"Yep."

Katherine rushed out of the living room, closed the pocket door, and bounded into the parlor. She was relieved to find Abby safe and sound on top of the window valance. "Come down, Abigail," she asked in a soft voice.

In one fluid swoop, Abby leaped to the fireplace mantel to the back of a chair, then sprang to Katherine. "Chirp," she cried.

Katherine picked her up, cradled the cat against her, and then hurried upstairs to the playroom. Iris was collapsed against the door, with her tail brushed out three times its normal size. "Yowl," she cried, terrified.

"It's okay, Miss Siam."

As Katherine opened the door, Iris flew inside. The other cats made a beeline for the door and struggled to get out, but Katherine put her foot up to stop them. "Back! Back!" she said. She studied the windows and was relieved there were no bullet holes in them, then carefully placed Abby inside, closed the door, and locked it. She dashed into her room and removed her Glock from the gun safe. Not wearing her waistband holster, she tucked the gun in the back of her jeans. Hurrying down the stairs, she moved to the atrium closet and pulled out a cat carrier. Walking into the room, she was surprised to see Salina holding her cat and singing to him in a sweet voice. Katherine recognized the tune as an old folk song, "Cotton Eyed Joe," but the teen sang it with different lyrics.

"I'm holdin' a cat named Wolfy Joe. He looks like a werewolf, don't you know." Salina looked up and giggled.

For the first time, Katherine noticed how emaciated the cat was. "Salina," she began gently. "Let's put him in the carrier. He might be happier there," then, "Are you hungry? Is Wolfy hungry?"

Salina nodded. "I'm hungry, but at my grandma's, Wolfy has been living off of bologna. Big Mama doesn't like cats and didn't have any cat food."

"Change of plans, my dear. Straight through that door, make a right. You'll end up in the kitchen. Make yourself a sandwich. The cat food is in a can in the cabinet next to the fridge."

"Yes, Ma'am, but can I hold him and not put him in the cage?"

"Sure, but once you're done in the kitchen come back here. Wait here until I get done talking to the police."

The teen moved to the kitchen, holding a very scared, skinny cat.

The sirens of the police and emergency vehicles echoed through the still night air and appeared louder because the falling snow muffled all other sounds. "It's about time," Katherine said gratefully.

Leaving the living room, Katherine slid the pocket door closed. She answered the front door to a very agitated chief.

"What the hell? I leave your house for a couple of hours and all hell breaks loose."

"I could say the same. What took you so long?" Katherine said, exasperated.

"For you, Ma'am, I'll explain." The chief assumed an official Chief of Erie voice. "We were ten miles out, north of here. There was an abandoned vehicle peppered with bullets stuck in a snow drift. It had rental car plates."

Katherine brought her hand up to her mouth. "Oh, no. Madison."

"You know the driver?"

Katherine didn't answer right away. She looked past the chief at the EMT personnel tending the dead man.

"Well?" the chief asked impatiently. "Tell me fast. Leave out the part about what you had for breakfast."

"Drive-by shooting. Black four-door sedan. Maybe a Cadillac. I couldn't see the driver, but I caught a glimpse of the man in the passenger seat. He wore a black sock hat, and had a close cropped beard."

"What color was his beard?"

"Black, I believe."

"Which one did the shooting?"

"The one in the passenger seat shot an automatic pistol. After he began firing, I couldn't see him because the gun's burst was blinding. Everything happened so fast. He shot the man who had just left my house."

"Okay, stop there." The chief yelled at Officer Troy, who was standing next to the EMTs. "Black four-door sedan, possibly a Cadillac."

"Shouldn't be hard to spot in this weather," Officer Troy answered.

"Notify the county and state boys."

"Yes, Chief."

A second Erie cruiser pulled in front and parked across the street. Two officers trudged over.

"Listen up, boys," the chief said in a loud voice. "This is a crime scene. I want the area taped off. Get Officer Mallory here to photograph the area."

An officer in his twenties, who had recently graduated from the police academy, asked, "Chief, what about the snow? It's covering the crime scene."

The chief glared at him. "I know that, Officer Daniels. I want you to canvas the area, talk to everyone on this block, and find out if anyone saw anything."

"Yes, Sir," Officer Daniels said, tramping in the direction of the yellow Foursquare.

"Not that house. No one lives there. I meant the house next to it, on the corner. Start there."

The officer nodded, and was clearly embarrassed by his fellow officers looking at him like he'd just said something stupid.

"Geez," the chief said in a low voice. "Dang rookie." Turning back to Katherine, he said, irritably. "Go on."

"A childhood friend showed up an hour ago. Her name is Madison Orson. She came inside, we talked for a bit, then Stevie Sanders showed up."

"What did Stevie want?"

"To ask me something."

"Ask you what?"

"I don't know. He didn't want to ask me in front of Madison, so we went into the living room. We were in there for a few seconds, when this man barged in."

"The deceased guy?"

"I guess. I didn't see him. We were behind the closed pocket door, but I heard him. He was angry. He began yelling at Madison and wanted to know if she'd asked me something."

"Seems to be the M.O. with you. What does everyone want to ask you?"

Katherine shrugged. "I don't have a clue."

Officer Troy joined the chief on the porch. "When the investigators are finished, the coroner wants the body taken to the hospital across the river."

"Excellent plan. Tell the coroner to call me when he gets there. I'll want to be in on this."

Officer Troy nodded, and walked back to the EMTs.

The chief noticed Katherine was standing in the doorway, shivering. "Go inside. We'll talk in there."

Standing in the atrium, Katherine resumed. "My friend drove a rental car from Indianapolis; a blue Toyota Corolla."

"Yep, a Corolla. The car was reserved by a man named Vinny Bellini. Do you know him?"

"No."

The chief pulled a small note book he kept in his back pocket, and flipped several pages. "He's from New York." He read an address in Brooklyn.

Katherine flinched. "That's close to where Madison lived when we were growing up."

"Finish the part about the shooting."

"The deceased, I mean Vinny Bellini — I assume it was Vinny Bellini because he rented the car," she digressed.

"Yes, yes. We've established that point. Then what happened?"

"Madison left after he did, but when she saw the sedan pull up, she stayed on the porch and hid behind a wicker chair. The shooter first fired on the rental car, then opened fire on the man. When the car sped off, Madison ran to Stevie's truck. I think she meant to steal it. I can't be sure."

"She probably figured the rental car wouldn't operate with all the bullet holes."

"Stevie's truck door was locked, so she got in the rental and left."

"Back up. Where was Stevie during this?"

"He chased after Madison and was livid that she was trying to get into his truck because his daughter was in there."

"Daughter? What was she doing there? Where is she now? She could be a viable witness."

"In my kitchen."

"Okay, enough for now. I want to talk to Stevie. I didn't see his truck. Where is he?"

"He left."

The chief threw his hands up, frustrated. "What the hell? Why?"

Katherine thought, but didn't say out loud, *He said he had something to take care of.*

Salina, who had been eavesdropping on the other side of the pocket door, slid it open and poked her head out. "My dad was looking for a place for us to sleep."

The chief recognized Salina from the many times he had to come to her trailer to arrest her mother. "I'm very sorry about your mom. I heard you're moving back to Erie."

"Yes, Sir. Dad bought the house next door and we came to see if this lady here," she said, looking shyly at Katherine, "would let us stay there tonight — before the bank did something."

Katherine added, "Salina, before the house closes. I'll talk to your father about this when he gets back."

The chief asked, "Salina, the man outside, did you see who shot him?"

"No," she said quickly. "I was hunkered down on my dad's floorboard. I saw a big black car, then I ducked."

Katherine looked at the teen, and wondered why she'd told her father who she thought it was, but not the chief. She'd ask her later. Instead she said, "Salina, can you slide the door closed and wait for me in the kitchen?"

Salina nodded and closed the door, but didn't leave the spot. She wanted to hear more about what the lady in the pink house was saying about her father.

"Finish your story," the chief encouraged.

"Stevie asked if he could leave Salina here for a while, and I said yes. That's all I know, but what about Madison? Where is she?"

"I don't know. Safe, I hope."

"Where did you say you found her car?"

"I didn't, but right about now it's being towed out of a ditch close to Chester's Snow Angel farm."

"That's off the highway, way out in the sticks. Why would she drive there?"

"I'm bankin' the two in the Cadillac were following her, and she slid off the road trying to get away from them."

"Why do you think that?"

"Tire tracks beside Madison's car indicate someone stopped by to help her."

"How can you tell?"

"Snow is like a blank canvas, and tire tracks in the snow are like fingerprints. They indicate whether the vehicle is a car or a truck." The chief tugged at his short beard. "We could see that only one person got out of the vehicle, and he had the biggest shoe size I've ever seen. It looked almost like a giant snatched her out of the car."

"I pray it was Chester. He's a big man."

The chief shook his head. "No, Katz, Chester is the one who called it in. Your friend exited her car and got into the other vehicle."

"Was there any sign of struggle?"

"None, so I'm hopin' a good Samaritan picked her up and took her to safety. I'm thinkin' a family, because Madison's footprints led to the left side of the other vehicle. She sat behind the driver. It was most likely a married couple, the wife riding shotgun. I expect to get a call from these folks soon. They'll want to know what to do with her."

"Chief, what if it wasn't a good Samaritan?" she worried.

"I hope, for your friend's sake, that whoever helped her wasn't the shooter."

Katherine buried her face in her hands. "This is terrible."

Chapter Twelve

Stevie drove into the parking lot of the Dew Drop Inn, and was quickly disappointed that his father's truck wasn't there. He had a hard time finding a space to park. The place was packed.

He walked into the smoke-filled bar, searching for someone he knew. A woman he used to date in high school sauntered over. "Hey, Stevie, wanna buy me a drink?"

"Sure, Loretta, what's your pleasure?"

"Are we talking about a drink or . . . "

Stevie shrugged off the innuendo. "If I remember, you like Bloody Marys." Stevie moved over to the bar. "Hey, Eddie, one Bloody Mary for the lady, and a Jack and Coke for me." Then to Loretta, pointing at the bar stool, "Ladies first," he said.

"Always the gentleman," she flirted, hopping up on the stool. "I never see you anymore. Where ya been hangin'?"

"I have a new business and it takes all my time," he answered, then said to the bartender, who had slid over the two drinks. "Where's my Dad?"

"He's in the back."

"But I didn't see his truck."

"Wrecked it headin' to Chicago. Rented a Cadillac."

Stevie tried to hide his murderous feelings.

Loretta said, slurring her words, "I wrecked my car last month."

Stevie ignored her. "Excuse me," he said, walking away. He headed for the back room, where his father, Sam, had his office. Sam was talking to two other men Stevie didn't recognize. "I need a word," he said abruptly.

Sam looked surprised. "Good evening, son," he said, then addressed the two men, "We're done here, right, fellas? I'll catch ya later."

The men got up, threw Stevie a curious look, and left.

"Shut the door," Sam yelled after them. One stepped back and obliged. After they left, Sam said, "Dave tells me you got your girl. I bet you're real happy about that?"

Stevie was so angry, he couldn't speak. The muscles in his neck contracted, then he spit, "That man you shot in front of Katherine Cokenberger's house wasn't Jake."

Sam got up from his chair. "What are you talkin' about?"

"Shut up, Dad. I know you put the hit on him, but to think you'd do it with Salina —your granddaughter — in the truck is so freakin' unreal, I can't believe you'd be so callous."

"You make no sense."

"What if Salina had been killed by one of those bullets?"

"I'm tellin' ya. I didn't do it."

"Eddie just said you wrecked your truck and rented a Cadillac. That's a four-door sedan, right? Is it black?"

"No, it's blue. Didn't you see it parked outside?"

Stevie began to realize his father might be telling the truth and didn't have a clue what he was talking about. He tried to calm down.

Sam came around the desk and stood next to Stevie. "Listen, son, I'll send out feelers about what happened, but you best get back to your daughter. Where is she? Is she outside in your truck? I know you didn't bring her in here."

"No, she's at Mrs. Cokenberger's house."

"Then, you get over there. Drive-by shootings don't happen in Erie for nothin'. Something ain't right."

"I'm leavin', but Dad, do you know anyone who uses an automatic pistol?"

"Fully automatic? Nope, not in my operation. Sounds pretty damn sophisticated. You go on now. Make sure Salina is safe."

"Thanks," Stevie said, leaving. As he headed out of the office and to the front door, Loretta called after him, "Ain't you stayin', sugar?"

"Another time," he said.

Chapter Thirteen

Early in the morning, after the previous night's shooting, Katherine walked into the atrium and picked up the handset of the landline phone. Scout leaped on top of the marble-top curio cabinet and tried to knock it out of her hand. "Get down," she scolded.

"Waugh," Scout cried haughtily, and leaped down.

"Is that butter on your face? You're not supposed to have butter."

Scout wiped her paw over her lips and licked it. She crossed her blue eyes and curled her lip, exposing one fang. "Na-waugh," she disagreed.

Katherine pressed the number of the Premier Hotel in Chicago, where Jake was staying. A friendly sounding robot answered, 'If you know the number of your party, please press the room number and then press the pound key.'

Katherine entered Jake's room number — 615 — and drummed her fingers on the curio, impatiently waiting for Jake to pick up. After seven rings, the call bounced back to the robot, which went through another annoying menu of options. "Oh, shut up already," Katherine said into the phone, pressing zero for the operator.

The front desk answered. A woman with a British accent answered. "Premier Hotel. How may I assist you?"

"Hello, my name is Katherine Cokenberger. My husband, Jake, is a guest at your hotel. He's in room 615. I've been trying to call him, but he doesn't answer. Is there a way I can have him paged?"

The woman laughed slightly, then continued, "We don't page guests. Why don't you leave a voice mail? The light on his phone will flash red; when he returns to his room, he'll see it and call you."

"I've left several voice mails. Listen, it's an emergency and I really need to speak to him. Can you at least have someone check his room?"

"No, I'm afraid that won't be possible. Here at the Premier Hotel, we respect the privacy of our guests. Hold on one second."

The woman put Katherine on hold for an unusually long time. Scout had returned to the curio table and was rubbing Katherine's arm, wanting to be petted. She reached down and kissed her on the back of her neck. "Sweet girl," she said into the phone, not knowing that the woman had returned to the line.

"Come again?"

"I'm sorry. I was talking to my cat."

"Oh," she said, without interest. Then, "I checked our guest register, and Jake Cokenberger is no longer staying at this hotel."

"What?" Katherine asked, spitting out the word in shock.

"It's against our policy to release over the phone when and what time our guests have checked out."

"I'm not just somebody. I'm his wife."

There was silence at the other end. Katherine tried a different tactic, "I have a power of attorney. Give me your fax number or an email address. I'll send you a copy of it. I demand to know when my husband checked out."

"No need to get snarky. He checked out at four o'clock a.m."

"No way," Katherine said.

"Thank you so much for calling. Have a pleasant day!"

"Just one second," Katherine said, irritated. "You've got the worst fake British accent I've ever heard. Maybe you should watch *Downton Abbey*!"

Katherine slammed the receiver down so forcibly that the phone fell on the floor.

Scout thought it was a game and pounced on the phone. Abra joined in. The two began wrestling for it.

"Give it to me," Katherine said, annoyed and worried. Retrieving the phone from the feisty cats, she said, "Cats, Jake is missing." A tear slid down her cheek. "Can you surf me up a clue where he is?"

"Ma-waugh," Scout cried, trotting off to the next room. Abra caught up with her and playfully smacked Scout on the back.

Someone knocked loudly on the door, and Katherine walked over to open it. "Margie, come in. I'm so worried. Jake checked out of his hotel at four o'clock this morning."

"But why, kiddo? Wasn't he supposed to stay until Sunday?"

"That was the plan. Why would he leave the hotel in the middle of a snow storm?"

"Makes absolutely no sense," Margie said, sitting down to remove her boots. "That wind is terrible."

"Did you drive over here?"

"No, I harnessed our yellow lab to a sled, and he brought me over," Margie joked. "Just kidding. Actually, I did drive. I know there's a state of emergency, but I've got to have food for my kids' breakfast. The police can go ahead and arrest me. Give me milk and no one will get hurt."

"You picked a good time to stop by. The last of the investigators have just left."

"I nearly had a wreck when I saw the crime scene tape. What happened? You're okay, right?"

Stevie Sanders walked out of the dining room, and stopped. "I thought I heard someone talkin'."

Margie fired a quizzical side glance at Katherine. Katherine put her hand up, and mouthed the words, "*Stop! I'll explain.*"

Margie said, "Hello, Mr. Sanders."

"Hello, Mrs. Cokenberger. Care for breakfast? I made enough to feed an army." Stevie smiled brightly.

"Thank you, but I'm on my way to the store to get some food. It better be open."

"Ma'am, don't waste your time. It ain't open. I mean, it *isn't* open," he corrected. "I checked earlier," he finished.

"I got groceries yesterday. What do you need? I can fix you right up," Katherine offered.

"Thanks, you're a lifesaver, but I bet you don't have my kids' favorite breakfast cereal."

"Probably not, but why don't you make them your famous pancakes."

189

"Yep, I can do that, but I'm out of syrup."

"Got ya covered."

Stevie cleared his throat. "Nice seein' ya. Got corn muffins in the oven." Stevie left. Iris followed him, nipping at his heels. "Hey, quit it," he said to the rowdy cat.

"Katz, what's going on?" Margie said in a suspicious tone.

Instead of answering, Katherine steered the conversation to Jake. "The last time I talked to Jake was last night, around six. He was off to a faculty dinner at a different hotel. I haven't heard from him since. He's not answering my voice mails. She quickly filled in Margie with the events of the previous evening, beginning with the fact that a friend she hadn't seen in years suddenly shows up at her front door.

Margie slowly began, "This is scary. I shudder to think that criminals in our town have guns that can fire like that. It has to be an outsider. Do you think it was a drug thing?"

"I have no way of knowing. The man who was murdered lived in my old neighborhood in Brooklyn, close to where Madison used to live."

"That's odd, with the millions of people who live in New York City. Maybe your friend fell for the guy next door. Just sayin'."

"Coincidence or naught, I hope the chief can find his family to let them know he's dead. I hate the fact that my house is such a murder magnet," Katherine said gloomily.

Margie gave a sympathetic look. "Hear. Hear. Let's change the subject. Why is Stevie here?" she asked nosily.

"It doesn't look like what it seems. Stevie showed up while Madison was here. He brought his daughter. They wanted to stay next door, but as you and I know, I haven't had time to order the furniture yet, so I offered to let them stay here."

"Oh, kiddo, I didn't mean to imply . . ." Margie's face reddened as her voice trailed off into silence.

*   *   *

Jake drove at a snail's pace on US 30 to Merrillville, Indiana, bumper-to-bumper in a long line of cars and semi-trucks. With the Jeep's tank nearly empty, he eagerly searched for a gas station. His eyes burned from watching the windshield wipers keep up with the snow, and his knee ached with pain from riding the clutch. He admitted to himself that he should have driven Katherine's vehicle. Spotting a twenty-four hour gas and convenience store, he parked in front of the closest available pump.

Several hours earlier, Wayne had nodded off. When the Jeep stopped, he woke up and looked around. "Where are we?" he asked sleepily.

"We're still on US 30, close to where Merrillville meets the interstate."

"How far is that from the hospital?"

"On a good day, that's about an hour and a half from the City."

Wayne looked at his watch. "Eight o'clock! We've been on the road for four hours! I must have really conked out."

"Pretty much. I think you could sleep through a tornado. The wind was buffeting the Jeep like a Tonka toy in front of a fan."

Wayne smirked. "I call a bathroom break," he said, getting out of the Jeep, and heading to the store.

"I'll fill the tank. Be there in a second. See if they have a pay phone, would ya?"

Jake filled up the tank, then parked in a space close to the door. A snow plow had pulled up and the driver got out. Jake approached him. "Hey, my friend's wife is in labor. He needs a ride to Lafayette. Can you take him?"

The driver looked suspicious. "Sorry, not allowed. It's against the rules. Listen, buddy, if I don't use the bathroom now, I'm gonna explode." The driver rushed off to the men's room.

Jake trudged into the store, noting that there was at least a foot of snow on the ground. He glanced around for a pay phone. Instead, he found something better — a kiosk with prepaid cell phones. He quickly bought one, and was about to punch in Katherine's number when the snow plow driver came out of the men's room. Jake followed him over to the coffee dispenser. Wayne came out and Jake motioned him to come over.

Jake began, "How's the Interstate?"

The snow driver filled his cup, then said, "Closed between here and Crown Point. It's hard to keep up, when the wind is gusting at forty miles an hour."

"What about south of Crown Point?"

"There's one Southbound lane open. I think the storm is pretty much done south of here." The driver put a lid on his cup and proceeded to the cashier.

Jake and Wayne walked after him. "Excuse me, Sir, this is my friend, Wayne," Jake introduced. "We were both in Chicago attending a conference. Now we're just trying to get back to our wives."

The cashier, a woman with gray hair, and in her late sixties said, "Ah, now, ain't that sweet."

Wayne interjected. "My wife is having our first child. I need to get to the hospital as soon as possible."

After the driver had paid and was heading to the door, Jake offered, out of earshot of the cashier, "We've been stuck in traffic for hours. I can pay." Jake took out a hundred dollar bill from his wallet.

The driver eyed it hungrily. "You wanna ride, too? The two of you?"

"If it's possible," Jake said.

"What about your vehicle?"

"I'm going to leave my Jeep here, then hire a flatbed towing service to pick it up when the weather gets better."

The driver said, "Okay then, hang on just a second. Let me see if I can get you boys back home." He got back into his cab, talked to someone on his cell, then powered down his window. "I can only get you to Crown Point. From there, you're on your own."

"That works," Jake answered.

"But I can't take both of you. Only one," he continued in a matter-of-fact tone.

"Wayne, you go."

Wayne was already removing his laptop from the Jeep. He yelled to the driver, "Is there a car rental place there?"

"Yeah, that's where I'm takin' ya."

Wayne turned to Jake, "Thanks. You're a good friend. When I get to the hospital, I'll make sure I call Katz and tell her what's going on."

Jake held up the new cell he'd bought. "I'm hoping I'll reach her first."

Wayne climbed into the cab and waved. Jake waved back. Jake stepped back into the convenience store to call Katherine.

Chapter Fourteen

The driver of the rented black Cadillac skidded on black ice and side-swiped a service pole that supplied electricity to a ramshackle farmhouse. The electrical line that ran to the nearby utility pole snapped in two. The light fixture hanging on the pole instantly turned off, enveloping the car in darkness. Only the headlight beams caught the heavy snow that swirled around them.

"Watch what you're doing!" Madison warned from the back seat of the car.

The driver slowly backed up. The passenger side of the vehicle buckled as he pulled away from the pole. He parked behind a dilapidated farm building, kept the engine running, and toggled on the overhead dome light. The snow was coming down so hard, he knew he had to find shelter somewhere. This was as good a place as any.

Madison demanded, "Dimitri, where are you taking me?"

The hitman riding shotgun leaned over his seat, and said menacingly, "Keep your mouth shut."

Dimitri, the driver and security guard of the jewelry store where Madison had worked, took the good cop role and spoke in a friendly voice. "No one will hurt you. Mr. Zhukov wants us to bring you back."

Madison tried to relax, clutching her fur coat around her. "If that's the case, then why are we parked out in the middle of nowhere?"

The two men talked in Russian. Dimitri pulled out his cell and talked to someone, then ended the call. He turned in his seat. "Boss says if you give us the package, we can take you back to — "

"Yes, I want to go home. I'm so sorry I made this mistake, but I didn't know what was in the package," she said. "It was addressed to me. I thought it was something I ordered online."

"No one is accusing you of anything. Give it back, and we go."

The hitman said to Dimitri, "Enough!" He opened the glove box, and removed an automatic pistol. He pushed in a magazine, and calmly — without any sign of emotion —turned and aimed the gun at Madison's head. "Give it to me."

"But I don't have it," she said, afraid for her life. This time she was telling the truth.

He swung his door open, got out and slammed it shut. Opening the back door, he slid over next to Madison, then closed the door. He began frisking her, searching her fur coat's pockets, patting her down, and then he reached across and snatched her tote bag. Dumping it unceremoniously on the seat, he began sifting through its contents.

Madison struggled to come up with a different story. "It's not in my bag."

"So where is it?"

"At LaGuardia, I didn't want to go through the airport's security X-ray with it, so I checked it in my baggage."

"Liar!" he stormed. "We didn't see any luggage. Where is the luggage now?"

"When Vinny went off to rent the car . . ." For the first time throughout her ordeal she started to cry. "Why did you have to kill him? He had nothing to do with this."

Dimitri comforted. "We're sorry for the misunderstanding. We thought he was armed. We were only trying to protect ourselves."

Through blinding tears, Madison said, "You're the liar! Vinny didn't have a gun."

"Enough," the hitman said. "Focus! Where is the luggage?"

"I don't know."

The man grabbed her by the throat.

"We're not playing a game here. Now!" he shouted.

Madison cried more, then said in a weak voice, "At my friend's house."

Chapter Fifteen

After Katherine helped Margie load up a few groceries, she returned to the house and walked back to the kitchen. Salina was finishing her breakfast, and asked to be excused so she could go to her room and check on Wolfy.

"By all means," Katherine said, taking a seat. "I know this is a silly question, but did you feed him this morning?"

"He won't eat."

"Salina, I have a doctor friend who specializes in cats. Can I take Wolfy to see him? If your dad says it's okay, you can come with me." Katherine looked at Stevie, who was now frying a skillet full of potatoes. Judging from the amount of dishes Stevie had prepared, Katherine wondered if he or his daughter hadn't eaten in days. Salina had eaten everything on her plate.

"Yep, Ma'am. Salina can go." Stevie turned back to the stove.

Salina toyed with her long braid, smiled shyly, and left the room.

Katherine lowered her voice. "Stevie, I think Wolfy is sick. My vet is very good."

"I don't have money to spend on that."

"How about a loan?" Katherine knew that many folks in Erie didn't take kindly to blatant charity.

Stevie nodded. "I'll pay ya back. Want me to drive you?"

"No, that's okay. I can make it in my Subaru. It's got four-wheel drive. As soon as the travel ban is lifted, we'll go."

"But first, I made something for you."

"You've got a smorgasbord of breakfast foods on the table. It's hard to choose."

"I didn't know what you liked."

"I didn't realize you were quite the gourmand."

"Somethin' I did in prison. I was a cook."

Katherine's eyes grew wide. This was a topic she didn't want to discuss. "Okay, then, I'd love some fried potatoes."

Stevie took the skillet off the fire, and scooped her out a plateful.

"What are those round things in it?"

"Cut up hot dogs. That's how my mama made it."

Katherine dove in. "Delicious."

Stevie asked, "Is it okay if I sit with you?"

"Yes, please do."

Katherine's cell phone rang. She didn't recognize the number that appeared on the top of her screen, but answered it anyway. "Katherine Cokenberger speaking."

"Katz, it's me," Jake said, relieved and happy to have finally reached her. "I've got so much to tell you."

"I do, too. Where are you? I nearly passed out when I found out you checked out at the hotel in the middle of the night. Why did you do that?"

"Wayne's wife is having the baby. She went into labor, and he needed a ride back to the city."

"Oh, my gosh. I'm so happy for them! Are you in the city?"

"No, I wish. I'm in Merrillville. The interstate is closed from here to Crown Point. In fact, a snow plow driver just whisked Wayne off, but couldn't take me."

"Are you checked in a hotel?"

"No, everything is booked solid. I'm at a convenience store. I'll have to wait it out until the road opens. The driver said I-65 is open south of Crown Point."

Stevie, not hearing the other end of the conversation, asked, "Does Jake need help?"

Katherine continued, "Stevie Sanders is here with his daughter. There was an incident at the pink mansion last night."

"What happened?"

"It's a long story, and I prefer to tell you in person."

"Why can't you tell me now?" Jake demanded.

"Because Stevie's daughter has a cat and he's very sick. I need to take him to the vet ASAP."

Stevie asked, "Is he stuck somewhere?"

Katherine put down the phone and said, "Yes, north of here."

"Let me talk to him."

"Jake, Stevie wants to talk to you."

"Put him on."

Katherine passed her phone to Stevie, who took it. "Jake, I can come and get you."

"You sure?"

"Yes, I ain't doin' anythin' else today."

"The road is closed from Crown Point to Merrillville."

"Maybe it will be open by the time I get there. If it isn't open, I know how to get around it."

"Thank you. I'm on US 30 at the Filler Up convenience store, about a half mile west of I-65. There's a restaurant across the street. I'm headed there now, and will camp there until you come."

"What's the restaurant's name?"

"Waffle Queen. Hey, thanks, I really appreciate this. Can you pass the phone back to Katz?"

Stevie obliged.

"Katz, I love you. Take care. And, make sure you give Stevie my cell phone number."

"You must have bought one of those prepaid ones."

"I did. Hanging up now. Kiss our kids."

"I love you, too," she said, hitting the end key. She turned to Stevie. "This is so kind of you. Let me check my travel app to see if the ban has been lifted in this area." She pulled up the app, read it, and smiled. "Houston, we are ready for lift off."

"I'll go upstairs and tell Salina what's goin' on."

"Oh, Stevie, before you go, do you have family near Merrillville?"

"Why do you ask?"

"I heard you say you knew a way around the closed Interstate. I'm just curious."

"Some things are better left unsaid."

Katherine nearly choked on her coffee. She realized Stevie must be referring to some criminal activity he had once been involved in that allowed him to find the back roads in the Merrillville area. "Sorry," she apologized.

"No problem."

*   *   *

Leaving Dr. Sonny's vet clinic, Katherine placed the empty cat carrier on the back seat of her Subaru, while Salina climbed up into the passenger seat. Taking her seat behind the wheel, Katherine carefully selected the words to explain to Salina that Wolfy was seriously ill. The poor girl had just lost her mother, then witnessed a violent crime. *Now her cat is not expected to make it*, she thought sadly.

Putting the SUV in reverse, Katherine said, "One time, a few years ago, one of my cats got very sick. She ate a poisonous plant. Dr. Sonny saved her."

Salina didn't comment, but asked, "Why did we have to leave him there? He doesn't like to be away from me."

Katherine drove out of the parking lot, and onto the highway. "Because he has a very bad kitty cold."

"But, when I catch a cold, I don't have to stay overnight at the doctor's office."

"Wolfy is also dehydrated. Dr. Sonny is going to give him fluids."

Salina was silent.

Katherine thought she didn't know what dehydration meant and explained. "Wolfy has a temperature, and because of his fever, he's lost a lot of fluid. He needs an IV to replace those."

"I know what dehydration means," Salina said sadly. "He hasn't been eating very much."

"Cats sometimes don't eat if they can't smell their food. With a cold, Wolfy wouldn't be able to smell whether or not the food was okay."

"How long does he have to stay there?"

"We'll call later and check on him, okay?"

Salina asked, "Where are we going now?"

"Back to my house. I've got something fun planned."

"Like what?"

"Like we pick out furniture for your new house."

"That won't be fun."

"Why?"

"Because Wolfy won't be with me . . . " Salina's voice trailed off.

"How do you know that?"

"Because I know he'll die." The distraught girl started to cry. "Because everything I love dies."

Katherine slowed down and turned off the highway into the driveway of a ranch house. Taking the girl's hand, she said, "I know you're worried. I am, too, but we've got to think positive, happy thoughts that Wolfy will be all right."

Salina gave Katherine a hard look. "I don't want to pick out furniture because my dad can't pay for it."

"He won't have to, because do you want to hear a little secret? Promise not to tell anyone?"

"Maybe."

"I'm buying it as a present. I want my new neighbors to have a fresh beginning. What better way than to have new furniture."

"You must be a millionaire."

"Well, sort of," Katherine laughed. Backing out onto the highway, she said, "Are you hungry? If the diner is open, want to grab a burger?"

"Yes, Ma'am." Salina's mood brightened at the mention of food.

*   *   *

No sooner had Katherine and Salina gotten back from the diner and inside the front door, the landline rang.

"Salina, go ahead and take your boots off." Katherine dashed to answer the phone.

"Katz, this is Dr. Sonny. I need to ask you this, and I didn't want to ask in front of Salina, but did any of your cats come into contact with Wolfy?"

Katherine had to think. "I can't be one hundred percent sure. The only cats that were out when Wolfy arrived were Iris and Abby, but they were in a different room. Since then, Wolfy has been locked up in one of my guest rooms. Why do you ask?"

"If Wolfy does have an upper respiratory infection, I can treat the secondary infection with antibiotics. However, keep a close eye on your cats. Usually, the incubation time for cats to catch the cold is two to ten days."

"What are the symptoms? What should I look for?"

"Eye and nasal discharge. Sneezing. Some cats cough. If any of your cats exhibit these symptoms, bring them in as soon as possible. I can prescribe meds for supportive care."

"Yes, definitely."

"Katz, bleach the area Wolfy was in: his bedding, the cat carrier you brought him in, and thoroughly wash any objects he may have touched. Spray the room with a good disinfectant and make sure your cats don't go in there for a while."

"You're scaring me. Do you suspect Wolfy has more than a cold?"

"We're running a blood test right now. Wolfy may have feline leukemia."

"Oh, no," Katherine gasped.

Salina walked into the room. "Is that my Dad?"

Katherine shook her head and raised a finger. "Just a sec," she said to the girl.

Returning to the phone, Katherine said shakily. "Yes, Dr. Sonny, please call as soon as you know something. Thanks."

"Salina, that was Dr. Sonny. He's doing a blood test to see how Wolfy's doing. He'll call us later with the results."

"You seem upset."

"No, I'm good," Katherine said, wanting to present a calm face to the teen. "Maybe we should check on the cats in their playroom."

"Can I come too?"

"Yes, of course."

Heading for the stairs, Katherine asked, "You know about germs, right?"

"Yeah."

"I need to move you to a different room. Do you mind?"

"Why?"

"Because Wolfy's germs could infect my cats."

"Oh, like how we catch a cold," Salina said knowingly.

"Yes, exactly. I need to clean the room. While I do that, would you like to hang out with the cats in the playroom?"

"Yes, Ma'am. My teacher said we should always wash our hands after being around someone with a cold."

"Your teacher knows best. Let's do that before we see my kids."

Salina giggled. "I think it's funny you call your cats kids."

"They are my kids — all seven of them."

"I'm gonna start calling Wolfy my fur kid."

"I bet he'll like that."

* * *

After thoroughly cleaning the guest room, where Salina and Wolfy had slept the night before, Katherine sat down on the twin bed and called Colleen. Her call went directly to voice mail, then Colleen called back several seconds later.

"Hey, Katz, Daryl told me what happened. I saw it on the morning news. Who is this guy?"

"A friend of Madison."

"What?" Colleen said, shocked, on the other end. "The saints preserve us. What's going on? Tell me true."

"For starters, when Mum gave Madison my address, who would have thought she'd fly out and visit me in a blizzard?"

"Oh, no she didn't. Start from the beginning."

"That *is* the beginning. Madison came over last night. She was acting really obnoxious, and totally out of character . . . well at least from the way I remember her —"

"Which is when we graduated from high school," Colleen finished.

"She only stayed for a few minutes. I left the room, and her male friend barged in and told her they had to leave. He left before she did, and got shot in front of my house."

"What was the motive? Daryl said the victim was from Brooklyn."

"He lived just around the corner from where you did, by the Italian Pub. I just don't get it. Why did Madison come to my house?"

"Surely when she first arrived, she must have said something," Colleen prompted.

"She said she was on her way to Chicago for a modeling job but her plane was rerouted to Indy because of the weather."

"Katz, I'm sorry my mum gave Madison your address," Colleen apologized. "She meant well, but — "

"I don't blame Mum for what happened, but if you talk to her before I do, please ask her to never give out my personal information. I've been a murder magnet since I've moved out here, and Mum knows that!"

"I will. So sorry. Hugs."

"No worries. I'll keep you posted."

Chapter Sixteen

When Dimitri, the Russian driver, parked behind an abandoned farm building, he didn't know he'd pulled into a viper's nest. He didn't see the black, extended cab pickup parked near the house. He would have if he'd not hit the utility pole and snapped the electrical cable, which immediately cut off the power to the exterior light to the property, and the electricity inside the house.

The property bordered Chester's Snow Angel farm, and was owned by Sam Sanders. Stevie's infamous father was negotiating a contract with an energy company to install their windmills. With the rental money he'd receive, he could ultimately go clean and give up his illegal drug business. But in the meantime, the decrepit farmhouse was Erie's crime boss's number one site for meth production, "cooking." Sam employed a skilled chemist with a degree from the university in the city. Sam offered an employment package few would refuse — shorter hours, with a higher salary.

The meth had been made and was waiting for distribution. The "cook," who was informally known as the Professor, sat on a folding chair facing three men: two were drug runners, and the third was Sam's son, Dave. When the electricity went out, the Professor yelled, "What the hell is goin' on?"

Dave stumbled to the window and looked out. "There's a black four-door sedan out there. Idiots have their dome light on. I see a man in front and two people in the back."

"Sounds like a government issue vehicle."

"Doesn't look like the Feds. If it were a bust, they'd be in here already."

"Let's go have a looksee," the Professor said, grabbing his jacket, black ski mask, and Smith & Wesson 9 mm handgun.

The other men were similarly attired and armed.

Dimitri turned in his seat and watched in horror as the hitman slapped Madison. "Stop!" he yelled. "Boss wants her alive." With the dome light blazing, lighting up the inside of the car, he didn't notice the group of men approaching the driver's side until it was too late to react. His door and the back passenger door were yanked open simultaneously.

The hitman reached for his weapon, and fired a volley of shots. One of them hit Madison in the side. She fell over to the left and collapsed against the door. She didn't scream. She didn't cry out. The pain was so intense, she remained silent.

Strong hands snatched the hitman out of the car and threw him in the snow. Another pair grabbed Dimitri as well.

"Tie his hands behind his back," Dave ordered in his thick Hoosier accent. The second man did so with plastic zip ties, while a third man pressed his boot on the hitman's back as a guarantee the Russian wouldn't put up a fight. "Get his gun. Boss would like to see that."

Sitting the hitman up, Dave said, "Nice gun. Got any more like that?"

The hitman spoke a chain of Russian.

"What's he sayin'?"

Dimitri, kneeling in the snow with the professor's handgun pointed at his head, translated, "He said his boss will pay you, if you let us go."

"Pay us? You're a damn foreigner. What kind of cash do you have on you? I get paid in American."

"No cash," Dimitri explained, "but the woman in back, she stole money from my boss. If we can get it back, we can share."

Dave now turned his attention to the back seat and looked at Madison. "Ma'am, is that right?" then he called out to the other men, "Hey, she's been shot. "That ain't no way to treat a lady," he said, kicking the hitman in the side.

Madison glanced in his direction. A tear escaped her eye and ran down her cheek. "Those men are Russian. They work for the mob. You don't want to piss them off."

"Is that a fact?" Dave asked facetiously, then in a venomous voice to the hitman, "We don't want your kind here. This is our territory."

Dimitri translated to the hitman, who suddenly veered forward and grabbed the legs of the drug dealer pointing a gun at him. They wrestled for the weapon. Dave and the other dealer joined in the fight. The Professor was momentarily distracted by the struggle, which gave Dimitri an avenue for escape. He dove for the driver's seat, floored the accelerator, and spun the car around. He drove at breakneck pace — swerving and sliding in the snow. The drug dealers shot several times at the vehicle, but only one hit the car. It fractured the back windshield.

Madison moaned from the back. "Take me to my friend."

Chapter Seventeen

It was getting dark. While Katherine paced the floor in front of the parlor picture window, Salina was upstairs camped out in the playroom. She'd finally exhausted herself and the cats, and the last time Katherine checked, Salina was sleeping on the larger cozy bed with Lilac and Abby snuggled against her. Scout and Abra were doing their evening reconnaissance mission and gradually got bored. They trotted into the parlor and jumped up on the windowsill to watch the snow fall.

Moving over to the cats, she petted their backs. "When is this snow ever going to stop?"

"Raw," Abra cried in a sweet voice. She nuzzled her head against Katherine's arm.

A few minutes before, Jake had texted that Stevie and he would be home soon, depending on road conditions. The interstate was open, but with restricted lanes. Stevie had picked him up without any difficulty. Once in the city, they made a quick detour to the hospital. Wayne and Leslie were the proud parents of a baby girl. He said that Stevie wasn't much of a talker, but he really appreciated the "rescue." Katherine could hear Stevie laughing in the background.

Looking out the window, Scout began to growl; Abra did the same. They stood up on their hind legs and dangled their front paws, doing their meerkat pose. Scout began wildly sniffing the air.

"What's wrong?" Katherine asked.

Scout cried a mournful "waugh." It sounded like a warning.

Staring out the window, Katherine saw a figure slide and stumble on the sidewalk. It fell down and then slowly got back up.

"Why on earth is someone taking a walk in this weather?" she asked out loud. "Cats, I've got to go outside and see if this person needs help."

Scout leaped down from the sill and threw herself against Katherine.

"Scout, what's the matter with you? I have to do this. I'll only be gone a minute."

"Na-waugh," Scout pleaded.

"Take Abra and go upstairs."

"Rawww," Abra cried in a plaintive wail.

Katherine gently pushed Scout aside. She ran to the front door and opened it. Madison fell in and collapsed on the floor. Blood was flowing from underneath her fur coat.

"Madison? Oh, no. Madison."

"Shot," she said with great effort. "Shut . . . "

Katherine closed the door and locked it. She grabbed her cell and punched in 911. "This is Katherine Cokenberger. Send an ambulance to my house. My friend has been shot."

Ending the call, she stooped down and spoke softly. "Who did this to you?"

Madison struggled to breathe, and whispered something.

"What did you say?"

"Run. Get out of the house."

"I can't leave you. The ambulance is coming."

"Give them the bag."

"What bag? Madison, did you leave drugs in my house? Is that what those men are after?" Katherine asked with grave concern. She instantly feared for the cats. *What if they found it?* She shuddered. *What if one of them ate something from it?*

"I'm sorry. I didn't mean . . . " Madison didn't speak anymore. She was dead.

Scout and Abra jogged into the small vestibule and began their death dance.

"Scout. Abra. Stop. Cadabra!"

The Siamese stopped and swiftly turned their heads toward the living room, with ears swiveled forward and erect. They both emitted a low, threatening growl. Abra hissed, Scout snarled.

"Stop it! Go upstairs, right now," Katherine commanded.

All three were startled by the sound of breaking window glass in the living room. The mansion's single-paned windows offered little protection against a determined criminal on the outside, trying to break in. The cats ignored the command and did exactly the opposite. They ran at breakneck speed into the living room.

Katherine removed the Glock from the back of her jeans. Her keen urban sense told her the two men who shot Vinny and Madison had come back, and were getting inside. She wasn't a trained law enforcement officer, and because she was a novice gun owner, she didn't want to face two gunmen who had automatic pistols. Katherine's theory about the number of intruders was wrong. Only one man was breaking in, the other was facing Sam Sanders's wrath in his back office at the Dew Drop Inn.

Gripping the gun with both hands, she backed toward the stairs, and said to the cats, "Treat! Treat!"

Abra ran out of the living room and nearly knocked her down, racing up the stairs.

"Scout," she cried.

Salina stood at the top of the stairs, holding a frightened Abby.

Katherine knew she had to get Salina and the cats to the attic. Their only chance of survival was to hide in the hidden staircase until the police got there. *Oh, dear God, please let the police get here first and not Jake and Stevie,* she prayed. Calming herself, she had to think of a way to get the cats to go into the attic. Dashing up the stairs, she gently took Salina by the arm. "Come with me. We've got to hide," she whispered. She led Salina to the attic door. Quickly unlocking the lock, she pushed her inside. "Go up and wait for me. I'm going to try and get the cats."

"Please don't go," Salina said, her voice quivering.

"Shhh! Please, be quiet as a mouse."

"Chirp," Abby agreed.

Stevie's daughter reluctantly climbed the attic stairs, and turned the corner to the first landing. Still holding on to Abby, she kissed the ruddy girl on the head. "I'll protect you," she said sweetly.

Katherine ran to the playroom and prayed the cats were still there and not investigating downstairs. To her relief, she found the cats sitting on their haunches at full attention. Lilac's fur was raised on her neck; Iris tail was brushed out.

Not wasting valuable time, Katherine hurried to the armoire where she stored the cat treats, yanked the bag off the shelf and opened it. The cats suddenly focused on the treat bag and not on the intruder sounds coming from the first floor.

"Treat! Treat!" Katherine called in a soft voice. She backed out of the playroom, and enticed the cats to follow her like she was the Pied Piper of Hamelin, but with one variation on the medieval theme: cats instead of rats. The cats trotted out of the playroom, led by Abra, with Lilac a close second. When the two Siamese noticed the door open to the no-cat-zone, the forbidden attic, they lunged for it. The kittens were slow in getting the memo. Dewey stopped, began sharping his claws on the carpet, and then looked up. Before he could belt out a loud "Mao," Katherine inserted a treat in his mouth. Iris, sensing the danger below, launched into her mother hen mode. Taking the rear flank, she nudged Dewey, and pushed Crowie with her paw. She drove the kittens like they were cattle, crisscrossing behind them and nipping at their backs until they were safe up the attic steps.

Knowing the door had noisy hinges, Katherine slowly closed the door but to no avail; it creaked loudly. Standing on the bottom step, she froze when she realized she couldn't lock the dead bolt from the inside. Frustrated and terrified, at the same time, she wanted to sit down on a step and cry. *Why do these terrible things keep happening to me? Scout's downstairs with murderers and I can't do anything about it, but I've got to save the others.*

Salina said in a frightened voice, "Ma'am, can we go now?"

Springing into action, Katherine snatched a flashlight off its hook, and directed the light in front of her. Salina stood wide-eyed on the landing, and was visibly shaking.

"It's going to be okay, Salina. Trust me."

Crowie began to meow his soft cry. Katherine picked him up and kissed him on top of his head. "It's okay, my darling."

Katherine hugged Crowie and placed him on her shoulder. Grasping the flashlight, she joined Salina on the landing. "I have a hiding place to show you. Get behind me and I'll show you where it is."

Katherine moved over to the beadboard panel; swung the metal plate aside, and pushed the key in the lock. She gave the key a hard twist, and the door opened. The cats rushed in the room, and began sniffing the torn up floorboard next to the secret trap door. Salina filed in behind the cats. Katherine inserted the key in the other side of the lock, pulled the door closed with the key, then locked it.

"Salina, hold my flashlight. I need both hands. Crowie, I'm going to put you down." She removed the kitten from her neck and set him down. Crowie ran to Iris, who began to wash his ears furiously.

"Mao," Dewey protested, wanting out.

"Shhh! Salina put Abby down and grab Dewey. You've got to keep him quiet."

A barrage of bullets rang through the second story of the house. Katherine gasped, "They're getting close."

Salina refused to let Abby go. She buried her face in Abby's fur. "How do they know we're here?" she cried.

"I don't know," Katherine whispered. She got down on her hands and knees, found the trap door latch, and pulled it up. She stepped down into the space and kicked open the secret wall panel. Returning, she said, "Salina, you come down first. Hand me, Abby."

"No, I'm not letting her go."

"Okay, hold her. Scooch to the side of the opening, let your legs dangle, and I'll pull you in."

Katherine helped her down, then crawled to the other end to make more room for the two of them. "There's a stairway landing through there," she pointed. "Take Abby and wait for me there."

"But it's dark in there."

"Here, take my flashlight. I'll be there as soon as I can."

"The cats? What about the cats? Gimme the treats," Salina improvised.

Katherine took the bag out of her pocket and handed it to Salina. Salina crawled through the opening to the landing and began shaking the bag.

The cats, thinking it was a game, hopped down and joined Salina on the landing. Lilac darted through the opening while Iris herded Dewey and Crowie in. Lilac me-yowled loudly. "Salina, keep them quiet," Katherine warned. She fished her cell phone out of her pocket and used the flashlight feature.

The "treat" trick didn't fool Abra. The former Hocus Pocus performer hesitated at the opening. "Come on, sweet girl," Katherine coaxed. She reached up to snatch her, but Abra escaped her grasp.

"Abra, no," she whispered. "Come here."

Climbing back up to floor to catch the defiant cat,

Katherine heard the sorrowful cry of Scout. So did Abra.

"I've got to save her."

Scout's sister cried a mournful "raw" and threw

herself against the beadboard panel.

"Stop it! You're going to hurt yourself."

Abra bashed into it again. Katherine grabbed her

with one hand and dropped her down into the hole. She

quickly placed the trap door on top, and moved to unlock

the beadboard panel.

Abra pulled herself up through the opening in the

damaged floorboard next to the trap door. The Siamese

waited for Katherine to open the door, then escaped. She

ran toward the attic stairs.

Katherine called with panic in her voice. "Abra,

no! Come back."

Chasing after Abra, she ran past the antique grandfather clock and snagged her sweater on the handle to the long, cracked glass door of the clock case. Stopping to unsnag her sweater, she looked up in horror as the clock rocked precariously on its cracked legs. Katherine reached up to steady it, but stopped when she heard someone below jiggling the door handle to the attic door. It jiggled once, then again. Slowly the door creaked open.

Katherine set her cell phone on the floor with its flashlight feature still on. She assumed her shooter's crouch. She held her Glock in both hands and aimed toward the door. It was pitch black in the attic except for the dim light of the cell phone. The advice of her gun instructor played in her head: "Only attempt to take an active shooter down as the last resort."

Poised to shoot, she placed her finger near the trigger. Waiting for the intruder to come up the stairs and turn the corner, she waited . . . and waited. Wondering what was taking so long, she started to get up when Scout slinked around the corner. "Waugh," the missing Siamese cried.

"Thank, God. Scout! Abra! Follow me." She picked up her phone and ran to the beadboard panel to the secret room. She mistakenly thought the cats were right behind her.

The seal-point sisters had other plans. They ran and squeezed onto the half wall, behind the grandfather clock.

"At-at-at-at," Scout clucked. She stretched up tall on her hind legs in the confined space behind the clock. Abra joined her. Their movements pushed the clock until it wobbled from back to front and then fell face-forward off the half wall. With a deafening crash, the clock blocked the stairs to the attic.

A man screamed in pain. "*Ya slomal nogu*," he yelled in Russian.

Katherine knew enough of the language to know the top-heavy antique had broken the intruder's leg. Scout and

Abra saved the day, or had they? *Where's his gun?* she wondered. *Where's the other guy?*

The man fired a round of shots through the space between the clock and the stairway wall. The bullets hit the uninsulated rafters of the attic.

"Go! Go! Go!" Katherine shouted to the cats.

The sound of police sirens filled the night air, and echoed throughout the empty attic. "Dammit, what took them so long?" she said, still worried. "Let Chief London deal with that nutcase Russian stuck on the stairs."

Beaming the flashlight around the attic, she called nervously to the missing cats, "Where are you?" Then Scout cried from the secret room, "Ma-waugh," which sounded like *hurry up and get in here.*

Katherine rushed in to find two impatient Siamese waiting for her, their tails whipping and thudding on the floorboards: *Thumpity. Thump. Thump.*

Katherine swung the door panel shut. "Okay, my treasures, let's join Salina and the other cats in the safety zone."

Securing the trap door over her head, Katherine crawled onto the landing where Salina was holding the cats. Lilac and Abby were on the teen's lap. Dewie and Crowie were vying for her shoulder. Iris sat several steps down watching the kittens in her protective mode.

"Oh, Ma'am, I'm so happy you came back," Salina said, with tears in her eyes.

Katherine sat down cross-legged next to her. Scout and Abra jumped on her lap and reached up to be petted. "Good girls," she cooed, then said to Salina. "Before we do a group hug, let's get one thing straight?"

"What's that?" Salina asked, bewildered.

"My name is Katz, not Ma'am."

Salina giggled, then became serious. "Katz, are we safe?"

"Yes, we are. One of the bad guys is pinned under a clock that weighs a ton."

"How did that happen?"

"Scout and Abra pushed a grandfather clock on him."

"You're joking. Cats can't do that."

"I saw it with my own eyes, but we better not tell anyone. They'll think we made it up."

"I guess the bad guy ran out of time," Salina said, and then put her hand over her mouth to smother a laugh.

"Ma-waugh," Scout agreed, and then scampered down the partial stairs.

"Have fun, Scout. Abra, you go, too," Katherine said with frustration. "Make sure you leap carefully at the place where the stairs are sawed off."

The cats stopped in their tracks, then padded back, eying Katherine curiously.

"I guess if I tell you two punks the opposite of what I want you to do, you'll do as I ask. Sound about right?"

"Raw," Abra cried, trotting over and head butting Katherine on the chin.

Chapter Eighteen

Stevie drove his Dodge Ram onto Lincoln Street. The entire block was filled with ambulances, an emergency fire truck, and several police cars. "This ain't a good sign."

Jake, riding opposite, opened his door and tried to climb out.

"Wait a minute, buddy. Let me stop first." Stevie pulled over, and jammed on the brakes. Jake got out and plodded through knee-deep snow on the not-shoveled sidewalk, then moved to the street, which had been plowed. Chief London stood on the porch of the mansion talking to an EMT. When he saw Jake coming up the front sidewalk, he said, "We can't find Katz or Stevie's daughter."

"What do you mean, you can't find her?" Jake asked with terror in his eyes. "She's not here?"

"No, we've checked everywhere, and can't find them. We were hopin' you'd heard from her."

"No, not since an hour ago. Stevie and I were in the city. We just got to Erie. What happened?" It was then that Jake saw the broken front turret window to the house. His eyes widened with horror.

"Let me give ya the short version. Katz's friend is dead, died in the front vestibule. Katz called it in. When we arrived on the scene, we found the broken window and Katz missing."

"So the shooters returned?" Jake asked. On the way back from Merrillville, Stevie had caught him up to speed with the details of the drive-by shooting.

"Only one," the chief said, pointing at the footprints in the snow on the porch leading to the window.

"Why's the fire department here?"

"We needed their help to remove a big old grandfather clock from our perp."

"What?"

"A Russian named Dimitri Godunov. He's got a serious broken leg. We've already taken him to the hospital, and are lookin' for someone to interpret. No one in Erie speaks Russian."

"Katz speaks a little," Jake said, then realized how stupid it sounded because Katherine wasn't there. "Did you check the Foursquare? The bungalow?"

"Nada, and she's not answering her cell."

Stevie ran up. "Where's my daughter?"

Jake reached over and touched Stevie's arm. "I think I know where they are. Chief, there's a back way to the attic. A few days ago, Katz and I found a secret access way, I mean, back stairs. Can Stevie and I go check it out?"

"Knock yourself out, but stay to the back of the house. I don't want you messin' up the crime scene up here."

"Thanks, Chief," then to Stevie, "We need to go to the basement back door, where Katz's classroom is. In the mechanical room, and under the stairwell, there's this heavy metal tool cabinet. We need to empty it out, and move it."

Jake started toward the back of the house. He moved down the slippery front porch steps two at a time. Stevie followed.

Jake filled in Stevie with the details of the hidden staircase, while Stevie listened quietly. Then Stevie said, "I bet they're there."

Cokey yelled from the front of the driveway. "What's going on?"

Jake motioned him to join them. He turned the key in the lock of the classroom door, then stepped down. Stevie followed, then Cokey, who was huffing and puffing from the exertion of running through the deep snow.

"Uncle, you've got to help us move that tool cabinet from under the stairs," Jake said.

"That big ol' thing? It probably weighs a ton. I'm surprised it survived the explosion," Cokey said, then bit his tongue. "Sorry, Jake, I didn't mean to say that."

"Whatever, but for starters, help me empty the blasted thing out. Oh, better yet, get me a step ladder. We're gonna need a tall one."

"I'll get the six-foot."

Chapter Nineteen

Sam Sanders sat behind his desk, facing the prisoner one of his drug dealers and son, Dave, had brought in through the back door. "Sit him down over there," he said, pointing to a sturdy, metal chair. "Cuff him to it." Then, to the prisoner, "Try anything funny and I'll . . . " He pretended to shoot the prisoner in the chest. The Russian understood the gesture, and nodded his head 'yes.'

"Folks around here don't take kindly to people like you shootin' up the town. My boys tell me you're here to get something someone stole from your boss. Something worth big bucks."

The Russian only understood half of what Sam Sanders had said. "*Da,*" he answered. "*Droga.*"

"You mean dope? What kind of drugs?" Sam asked.

The Russian gestured shooting a needle in his arm.

"Heroin?"

"*Da,*" the Russian answered.

"Well, Mr. — what's your name?"

"Vladimir."

"Mr. Vlad man, we don't want that kind of dope around these parts. We don't want you sellin' in our territory, either, got that?"

The Russian started to get up from the chair but the handcuffs held him back. Dave hit him on the head with his revolver. "Back off, buddy," he said firmly, then to his father, "What should we do with him? Lady in the car said he was the Russian mob."

Sam leaned back in his chair and put his feet up on his desk. He placed his hands behind his head. "Well, now, son, we definitely don't want to kill him. We'd have those Russian boys coming down on us in larger numbers, so why not drive him to the Indy airport and put him on a plane?"

"I can do that, but I'll need to take a few guys with me."

"Yep, for insurance."

"What about his gun?" Dave asked.

"I think I'd like to have it. Don't have one in my collection."

"Now you do," Dave said, pushing the automatic pistol across the desk.

Sam spoke to the prisoner. "So, you go bye-bye now." Sam stuck his arm out and waved his hand, gesturing a plane flying in the air. "And don't come back. If you do . . . " Sam gestured a gun being fired at the Russian's head. Borrowing a line from a mafia movie, he said "Bang, you're dead."

Chapter Twenty

Jake, Stevie, and Cokey moved the heavy cabinet aside from the wall under the basement stairs, revealing the opening at the bottom of the hidden stairwell. Jake positioned the six-foot-tall step ladder inside the space, and called up from below the sawed-off stairs. "Katz, are you up there?" He climbed up three of the ladder rungs, and shone his flashlight upward on the bottom step.

"Yes," Katherine answered happily. "I'm with Salina and the cats. We're coming down."

Katherine stepped down the stairs, with Salina close behind. She was holding two cats, Iris and Dewey, while Salina held Abby and Lilac. Scout and Abra passed them on the stairs and darted down the rest of the way. On the bottom stair, they eyed the step ladder, and vied for the best position to jump onto the painter's shelf. Crowie beat them to it. The kitten soared through the air and landed on the very top.

"You little monkey," Jake said, grabbing the cat, and placing him on his shoulder. Crowie shifted to the other side of Jake's shoulder, and made himself comfortable by digging his claws into Jake's wool pea coat. "Stay there, little man. Don't jump down."

From the cut-off stairs, Scout gracefully leaped on the top cap of the ladder, then Abra joined her.

"Baby girls. Stay," Jake commanded.

"Na-waugh," Scout sassed. In a single bound worthy of Superman, Scout and Abra leaped down, and scampered out from underneath the stairwell, and into Katherine's classroom.

"Scout! Abra!" Katherine yelled, then muttered, "They do what they want to do."

Jake beamed his flashlight up the stairwell.

Katherine appeared with a wide grin on her face. "You are a sight for sore eyes," she said, then to Salina, "You better sit down on a step. I don't want you to fall."

"Where's my dad?" Salina asked excitedly.

"I'm right here," Stevie said, walking over, and standing at the foot of the step ladder.

Jake said, "Katz, I was worried sick something awful had happened to you. Why didn't you call or text me?"

"I turned my phone off. I didn't want the crims to hear it ring or ping when I got a text message."

"It was only one criminal."

"Great," Katherine said dejectedly. "That means the second one is still at large."

"Afraid so, but Chief London is working on it. We've got to put the cats up somewhere. They can't roam the house. The front turret window is broken."

"From the awful sound of breaking glass, I figured it was one of the three," Katherine said.

"I'll fetch a couple of cat carriers," Cokey announced. "Katz, are they still in your office closet?"

"Yes, but before you go up there, can you catch Scout and Abra and lock them in the powder room? We don't want them to get out of the house," she warned.

"I'll try, but I can't guarantee they'll let me catch 'em," Cokey said, leaving.

"Thanks," she called after him. "Jake, let Salina come down first."

"Okay," he answered, then asked Stevie. "Hey, can you steady the ladder?"

"Yep, don't mind if I do," Stevie said clutching the ladder's side.

"Salina, hand me Abby, then Lilac."

Salina carefully placed each cat in Jake's hands.

Jake carefully climbed down to the bottom of the ladder, and called up to Salina. "Swing your legs over, then let your foot find the second step from the top of the ladder. Step down and hold on to the top."

"I've been on a ladder before," Salina said. She followed Jake's instructions and climbed down the ladder. She bounded toward Stevie.

"Baby cake," he said. "Daddy is so glad to see you're okay." He gathered his daughter in his arms and kissed her on the top of her head.

Salina said animatedly. "You won't believe Katz's cats. They are so smart," then to Jake, "I can hold Abby and Lilac again."

"Thanks, Salina," Jake said, handing her the cats.

"Chirp," Abby cried sweetly. Lilac belted a happy me-yowl.

Stevie looked up at Katherine and flashed a smile of gratitude. "Thank you, Ma'am, for taking care of Salina."

"You're welcome," she smiled back, then handed Iris and Dewey to Jake.

Cokey returned with the cat carriers and set them on the floor outside the stairwell. Jake opened the grilled metal front door of the first one and placed Iris and Dewey into it, then he removed Crowie from his shoulder and put him in there, as well. Salina handed him Abby and Lilac. He placed them in the second carrier, then he headed back to help Katherine climb down the ladder. Once she'd stepped off the ladder, he hugged her.

Katherine buried her face in his chest. "How was your day?" she asked for want of a better thing to say.

"I've had better," he answered.

Chief London clumped down the stairs from the first floor office to the basement. "I see I'm just in time for the rescue moment. Katz, are you okay?"

"Yes, Chief. I'm good," she said, stepping away from Jake. "Salina is okay, too."

"Are your cats okay?" he quizzed.

"Yes. I was very worried that one of them took a stray bullet, but I've checked them. They're fine."

"Well, you must know that one of them did a number on our perp."

"How is that?" Katherine asked.

"He's got a big scratch down the front of his face."

"Maybe he got cut on the glass," Katherine offered, deliberately not mentioning that Scout and Abra were in the same room with the intruder when he broke into the house.

"Or maybe one of your cats scratched him. Should I bag their paws for evidence?" he asked with a playful glint in his eyes.

"You're not going to arrest my cats, are you?"

"What would the charge be — assault with an antique grandfather clock?" Then, he slapped his knee and started laughing.

Salina started giggling. "Dad, time caught up with the bad guy."

The chief ran his hand through his hair. "That's a good one. Well listen up, folks. No one is staying here tonight. Katz, I suggest Jake and you go to your bungalow."

"Okay, that can be arranged," she answered. Then to Stevie, "Salina told me why you came to my house. Yes, you can stay in the Foursquare before the closing, but tonight, Jake and I want you to stay with us at the bungalow. We have a guest room for Salina and in the living room there is a fold-out sofa bed for you."

"Oh, Ma'am, that's good of you to offer, but —"

Salina finished, "We'll be happy to stay with you."

Jake said, "Yes, I can vouch for Stevie and me. We are both bone-tired."

Stevie answered, "But I'm not too tired to grill everybody a big steak."

The chief asked with a twinkle in his eye. "Where ya gonna get a steak in this kind of weather?"

Salina answered. "I checked out Katz's fridge. It's loaded with steaks."

"Salina," Stevie lightly admonished.

"Let's go!" Katherine said, now holding Jake's hand. "Let's gather up our stuff, the cats, and head on over to the bungalow."

"Ma-waugh," Scout cried from behind the door of the powder room. "Raw," Abra added, which sounded like *I second that.*

Cokey said, "If Margie and I whip up some sides, can we come too?"

"Yes, you are quite welcome. Bring Tommy and Shelly, too. Chief, would Connie and you like to come?" After she'd asked the chief, she wished she could retract her words. She had created work for the chief, thanks to Madison and the intruder. She suddenly felt very sad her childhood friend was dead, and wished she could have done something to prevent it from happening.

The chief caught her change of mood. "Katz, I'll talk to you later. You take care now, ya hear?" He quietly left through the classroom exit door.

Chapter Twenty-One

A day later, and back at the mansion, Jake and Katherine sat in the kitchen at the glass-topped Parsons table with Detective Linda Martin, an investigator for the Indiana State Police. The detective hadn't come for a social call. Her job was to collect as much information as possible about what had transpired at the pink mansion. She opened her laptop, keyed in her username and password, then looked up. "Katz, I've read your complete transcript regarding Madison Orson. Is there anything you wish to add?"

"Not really except Madison's personality was radically different from when I knew her."

"How so?"

"It was like she had been invaded by a body snatcher."

Jake laughed nervously. "Yeah, I saw that movie. I liked both versions."

"What I mean is," Katherine began. "Madison didn't seem to be the same person I knew growing up. She'd changed so much. I didn't recognize her." She paused, then added, "I feel sorry I wasn't there for her. Maybe if I'd kept in contact, her life would have turned out differently."

Detective Martin said, "There's an old proverb my mom used to say, 'Hindsight is better than foresight.' Katz, you can't be held accountable for another person's behavior. Madison made some wrong choices — the last one got her killed."

Jake reached over and took Katherine's hand in his. "Sweet Pea, don't beat yourself up over what you could have or should have done. The past is a done deal. Let's move on to the future."

Detective Martin continued, "From what I've gleaned from our investigation, Madison was heading to Chicago to assume a new identity. We found several counterfeit driver's licenses in her bag."

Katherine asked puzzled, "How did she get them?"

"Bogus licenses are being produced overseas and sold online. The best fakes look incredibly real. Some are blanks onto which photos can be added. You can buy them for about a hundred fifty bucks."

"Incredible."

"There was a case in Illinois where fake licenses were mailed from China to a bunch of students, inside a tea set."

"What happened to the students?" Jake asked.

"Many were kicked out of school. Plus, their real driver's licenses were suspended for a year."

"Who did Madison know in Chicago?" Katherine asked. "Was there anything in Madison's bag — an address book, a contact list on her cell — to point to a person you can talk to? I know she had a cell, because the first time she came to my house, and after I'd locked up the cats, she was texting someone."

"We didn't find a cell phone. I combed through the items in her bag. Nada. Only personal items; she had over a thousand dollars in cash. A few credit cards. The fake driver's licenses, of course. This is a long shot, but did she have family in Chicago?"

"Not that I know of. Madison's father left her mom when Madison was a baby. Her mom passed away a few years ago. That's it. No brothers. No sisters."

"I've been dabbling in the psychology of the criminal mind. What was Madison's mother like?" the detective asked.

"Sweet as pie," Katherine answered. "She worked very hard to take care of herself and Madison. I loved her."

The detective shrugged. "Well, we can't blame genetics. I'm waiting to hear from the New York City Police. They're searching Madison's apartment for clues. Particularly, I want to know if there was a person in Chicago she was meeting."

"If she was meeting up with someone in Chicago, why ask Vinny Bellini to go with her?"

"Katz, from the way you described her, Madison needed to be the center of attention at all times. She needed the attention from others to help support her ego."

"It's probably not my place to ask this question, but did you get a hold of any of Vinny's relatives to tell them he's dead?"

"It's okay for you to ask that question, but what I'm about to tell you is in the strictest confidence."

"Of course."

"Scout's honor," Jake held up his hand in the official Boy Scouts' gesture.

Scout heard her name and trotted in. "Waugh," she cried, in-between yawns. Jake patted his lap, and Scout jumped into it. He began stroking her back. She crossed her eyes and stuck out her pink tongue.

Detective Martin asked, "Is this the Siamese that got outside after your wedding ceremony?"

"Yes," Katherine said, "And, under the circumstances, and how she saved me, I'm so happy she did."

"Smart cat, that one," the detective offered, then returned to the topic at hand. "Vinny's father said his son had recently started dating Madison. They had been friends, off and on, for years, but only in the past month, things had heated up between them."

Katherine shook her head. "She didn't care for him. She used him to get out of NYC."

"Just a guy wantin' an adventure," Jake added. "Poor fool. Didn't have a clue what he was getting into."

"Back to you, Katz, why do you think Madison didn't care about Vinny?"

"Because after Vinny got shot and the shooter was out of the picture, she didn't check to see if he was still

268

alive. I remember when Jake was shot, I freaked out. Madison was a cold, callous person."

Jake hugged Katherine. "I know, Sweet Pea."

Katherine looked at him adoringly.

"Ma-waugh," Scout interjected, purring loudly.

Jake smiled, then asked, "Just out of curiosity, did Vinny have a criminal record?"

Detective Martin shook her head. "Clean. The NYPD couldn't find anything on him. Not even a traffic ticket."

"What about Madison?"

"Several arrests for cocaine possession. Petty theft. Shoplifting."

"The Madison I knew would never have done anything like that."

"We've been able to trace where Madison bought her airline ticket, from LaGuardia to Chicago O'Hare, with the reroute to Indianapolis. She ordered it online at her place of work."

"A modeling agency, right?" Katherine asked.

"No, she was a receptionist at a jewelry store."

"Oh, that's right. Colleen told me that her mother ran into Madison on the street, and she said she was temping on 47th Street."

Detective Martin noted, "That's something you didn't mention in your police report."

"I'm sorry, it just came back to me."

"Anything significant about 47th Street? I've never been to New York."

"The area between Fifth and Sixth Avenues on Forty-Seventh Street is known as the diamond district. It's the world's oldest and largest diamond exchange. I know this, because I worked very close by, and would often go there, walk the street, and do window shopping."

"Ouch," Detective Martin said. "Something just bit me."

Katherine and Jake looked under the table. Iris sat close to the detective. The Siamese blinked her eyes, and assumed an innocent look.

"Iris," Katherine scolded. "Get over here." She lifted up the misbehaving cat and sat the Siamese on her lap. "I must apologize for Miss Siam's bad behavior. I don't know what has gotten in to her."

"Yowl," Iris cried.

"A little less sass would be appreciated."

"It was just a nip. It wasn't like an alligator bit me," the detective chuckled. "Where's the other cats?"

"Toasting their buns on the office floor register."

Jake questioned. "What about the Russian who broke into our house?"

"No two ways about it. He broke into your house, and ended up with a broken leg. Katz, is it really true, two of your cats pushed a heavy grandfather clock on the man?" the detective asked skeptically. "The chief said there were paw prints in the dust on the back of it."

Katherine nodded. "But you've got to understand, the clock was very dangerous. I was in the process of hiring someone to dismantle it and take it out."

"How did your cats know this?"

Katherine answered honestly. "I truly don't know."

"Okay, back to the Russian. Right now, he's being held at the Erie jail."

"What's the charge?"

"Unlawful entry."

"And not murder?"

"We have no evidence to suggest he was the shooter. We bagged his hands and no gun residue was found."

"I'm still unclear how he and Madison made their way to my house," Katherine said.

"Somehow the driver was able to ditch the shooter, and he drove Madison back here to look for something she left behind."

"She said 'give them the bag.' I don't know what she was talking about. I know she wasn't referring to her purse because she took it with her when she left the night before."

The detective continued, "I assume the driver knew Madison was gravely injured. He didn't care enough about her welfare to take her to the hospital or to see her safely in your house. When he realized you had locked the front door, he chose another way to get inside."

"By breaking a curved glass window that will be difficult to replace," Jake offered.

"Your uncle Cokey is a fast worker. I noticed when I came in he already had plywood up to cover the window."

"Jake helped too," Katherine added.

"Let's back track a little," the detective said. "First of all, the man's name is Dimitri Godunov. He barely speaks English, so we were lucky to find a Russian language professor at the university in the City. Katz, do you know this man?"

Confused by the question, Katherine answered, "I don't know either one of them. Should I?"

"I'm referring to Mr. Godunov. I was able to interview him a few hours ago. He seems terrified of something. Actually, he's scared stiff. I requested a psychologist to check him out."

"Terrified of what? Of being arrested?"

"I'm thinkin' something else."

Katherine said knowingly, "He probably has mob connections, and he's afraid of repercussions because he failed to do whatever he was hired to do."

"What do you mean?"

"In New York City, the Russian mob has been around since the Soviets let them out of the old USSR. Maybe even before that."

"When?"

"In the 1970s. Russian Jews were allowed to leave, and they did so by the thousands, but the government also let out of prison a lot of criminals, who ended up in the United States."

"Interesting way to get rid of your unwanted prisoners," Detective Martin said.

"No, not your average criminal, but worse. Hardened criminals. Murderers."

"Katz, you amaze me with your insight. How do you know this?"

"I grew up close to Brighton Beach. It's on the tail end of Brooklyn, close to Coney Island. When you live in a big city like New York, your street sense develops very fast. Everyone is said to be very afraid of the Russian mafia."

Jake asked, "Why just the Russian mob?"

"Unlike other mob organizations who take care of business by assassinating individuals, the Russian mob targets entire families."

"Good lead, Katz. I'll pursue it."

The cats in the next room became very vocal. One of them was batting a large marble around. It rolled on the floor, bounced on the wall, then made its way into the kitchen. Abby bolted in, pounced on the marble. She pawed the toy with her left foot and with her right paw gave the toy a croquet-style whack. It skidded off one of the cabinets, angled to the table, bounced off the leg, and came to a stop on Detective Martin's shoe.

She laughed, "Hockey! My cats play it all the time with a ping pong ball." She reached down to pick up the toy, then said in a shocked voice. "Eureka moment, folks. I'm ninety-nine percent sure why Madison told you to 'give the bag to them.' The pieces of the puzzle are falling into place." She sat back on her chair, clasping the toy in her hand.

Katherine and Jake exchanged curious glances. "How is our cat's marble relevant to the case?"

Detective Martin slowly opened her hand. A large, brown gemstone gleamed in the light of the lamp near the table.

"Is it real?" Katherine asked, shocked.

"Let's find out. Katz, could you please get me a glass?"

Katherine got up, walked over to the cabinet above the stove, and pulled out a small drinking glass. She returned to Detective Martin and handed the glass to her.

The detective took the diamond and easily put a visible scratch on the glass. "Oh, I'd say that it's very real. This is a brown diamond. Most come from Australia. You've probably seen TV commercials for 'chocolate diamonds.' Judging by the size of it, I bet it's worth a great deal of money."

"The cats have been playing with it for days. I thought it was their marble," Katherine said, astonished.

Jake added, "Usually the cats prefer the uneven floor in the living room. I'm surprised it made its way out here."

Detective Martin got up from her chair. "Let's go in there and check it out."

"Do you think they're more?"

"Correct me if I'm wrong, but Madison said 'bag.' At first, I thought she was talking about drugs."

"Me, too," Katherine agreed.

"A jeweler's bag can hold more than one diamond," Jake added.

Katherine stifled a laugh. "A search and rescue mission for diamonds."

The trio walked into the living room with a group of inquisitive felines trailing behind them. Iris sat guardedly in front of the famous winged back chair, where Abby and she hid their loot.

Katherine gave Jake a knowing look, got down on her hands and knees, and felt inside the torn lining of the chair. An assortment of missing — stolen — objects rained out and fell to the wood floor.

Detective Martin was amused. "Kleptocats," she said. "It's a new word for the Webster's dictionary."

Jake said, shifting through the stuff, "We've got a shoe lace, pink ladies razor, fortunately with the safety cap intact, one very soiled T-shirt stolen from the laundry, and a chewed-up credit card case." He opened it, did a cursory glance, then handed it to the detective.

She eyed it curiously, and removed a credit card. "This is interesting. Katz, it has your name on it. Better call this bank ASAP."

"Where Madison is, I don't think she'll be using it," Katherine said tight-lipped, taking the card and putting it in her pocket.

Dewey and Crowie leaped inside the torn lining and began tussling. "Mao," Dewey exploded. Crowie hissed; Dewey growled.

"Come out, little men," Jake said, dragging out the playful cats.

Iris — always the over-protective adopted mom — trotted over and grabbed Dewey by the nape of his neck. She then began grooming him.

Detective Martin asked, "Are there any other chairs the cats hide things in?"

Abby sat on top of a fancy-scrolled floor register, looking like a regal Egyptian goddess. "Chirp," she cried proudly.

Jake moved over and picked her up. "Whatcha got there, baby girl?"

Katherine pried up the register cover. Using the flashlight function of her cell phone, she shone the light inside the register. Carefully, she pulled out a tattered organza jeweler's bag with numerous diamonds gleaming in the light. The satin ribbon closure was chewed, and the top of the bag was missing, but the bottom of the bag was intact.

"Hand it to me," Detective Martin said. She tugged a plastic evidence bag from her jacket, and set the torn bag inside. "Let's head back to the kitchen. I want to do an Internet search on recent New York City jewel thefts."

Still holding Abby, who was purring loudly, Jake followed Katherine and Detective Martin back to the kitchen.

The detective pounded several strings of search terms, and spent several minutes doing this. "No matches. I'm going to step into the next room. Excuse me," she said, getting up. "I need to call the NYPD and ask if any jewelers in Manhattan have reported a theft as big as this." She walked into the next room.

Katherine whispered to Jake, "She's going to come back and say there wasn't any theft report."

"Why do you think that?"

"Well, because if the diamonds came from a legitimate jewelry store, the owner would report it to the NYPD. News reports of the heist would be blasted on television, the Internet and in newspapers. I read the *New York Times*. I haven't seen anything mentioned about missing diamonds."

"We know the cats stole the diamonds — "

"From Madison's tote bag."

"Personally, I don't think they stole them to solve a mystery. They just wanted to play with them," Jake noted.

Katherine gave an inquisitive look. "You think so?"

Jake set Abby on the floor, who leaped up to the countertop to the top of the window valance, then ran its full length. "Let's think of clues. Why was my dirty t-shirt in the infamous chair?"

"Chirp," Abby cried guiltily.

"Don't forget Don Henley's song, 'Dirty Laundry.' I've walked into my office several times and that song was playing on YouTube. Madison made the mistake of stealing from the wrong person. I suspect the jewelry store owner was selling diamonds that were purchased with dirty money from criminal activity."

Detective Martin came back in. She'd overheard the tail end of Jake's and Katherine's conversation. "Yes, Katz, I think you're right. The NYPD has received no reports of a jewelry store heist. I suspect money laundering, as well. I've notified the FBI."

"Come again? How is this whole thing related to money laundering?" Jake asked.

The detective answered, "The mob makes money illegally, they send it electronically overseas, there it is used to buy diamonds. The diamonds come back legitimately to the US, and the jewelers sell them. Simple."

"So, I assume the FBI has the address of Madison's employer. I hope there'll be an arrest made there soon," Katherine said.

"That part is out of my hands, but in Erie I have a few loose ends to tie up." The detective returned to the table and gathered up her laptop. "Katz, always a pleasure talking to you. And, you too, Jake. Take care of those fur kids," she said, leaving.

Katherine and Jake followed her to make sure the front door was locked. Katherine hugged Jake around the waist and looked up at him. "I hope this is the last time we'll see dirty laundry in the wing back chair."

Jake leaned down and kissed her on the head, "I expect my T-shirts are safe for now."

"I wonder what happened to the second Russian — the shooter?"

"If he's smart, he'll surrender to the FBI, and rat out the members of the mob, then go into the witness protection program."

"That's not a happy thought, especially since he shot Madison."

"Katz, we don't know that. But it's scary that a criminal can be protected by our government."

"Hitmen have entered the program many times."

285

"History often repeats itself."

"Yes, Professor."

"Waugh," Scout agreed, sitting on her haunches nearby. She crossed her blue eyes in an insane expression, then lifted up her back leg and began washing it. Her pink tongue darted in and out, between her toes.

Chapter Twenty-Two

Katherine threw on a warm coat, stepped into her boots, and pulled on a sock hat. She walked to the Foursquare, climbed up the front steps, and rang the doorbell. She'd texted Salina earlier that she was coming. She'd bought Salina a cell phone so that the teen could always call or text if she needed anything.

Salina opened the door and said happily, "Katz, come in. I want you to see the new furniture."

Katherine cast her eyes around the living room, which was graced with comfortable mission-style furniture. "Wow," she admired, then asked, "Where's your dad?"

"He's working today."

"On Sunday?"

"Yes, he said he had to get caught up. He's an electrician, you know."

Katherine nodded. She marveled at how well-spoken Stevie's daughter was. And smart.

Wolfy padded in and rubbed against Katherine's legs. "Glad to see you're a lot better," she said, reaching down to pet him, then thought *I'm so relieved, in more ways than one, that he tested negative for feline leukemia.*

"He hasn't sneezed in days."

"I'm glad to hear that. Oh, and by the way, my kids didn't catch the cold."

"I know."

"How do you know?"

"Wolfy told me." Salina looked very mysterious, then burst out laughing. "I'm kidding."

"How does Wolfy like the new food Dr. Sonny prescribed?"

"He wolfs it down," Salina laughed again.

Katherine smiled. "He'll look grand when he's back up to his normal weight."

"And, no more bologna."

"Listen, Salina about our little secret, does your dad know I bought the furniture?"

Salina shook her head. "Nope, that's our secret forever and ever and ever."

"Who does he think bought it? I'm just curious."

Wolfy meowed softly and reached up for Salina to hold him. The teen scooped him up and kissed him repeatedly on the top of his head. "Love, love, love you," she said, then answered, "He said he thought grandad bought us the furniture as a peace offering."

"A peace offering? For what?"

"Oh, my grandad and my dad don't see eye-to-eye."

"I kinda knew that," Katherine said.

"Dad said he took out an insurance policy with my grandad that something bad would never happen."

"An insurance policy? How?"

"I don't know. I'm just telling you what my dad said."

"Salina, an insurance policy can protect you in many ways. In return, you pay a premium." She worried what Stevie had promised in return.

"Oh, my grandad is going to make sure all of us are safe in our houses, that there will never be a drive-by shooting again."

Salina's comment made Katherine think of the day Sam Sanders and his daughter Barbie returned Iris, who had been missing for several weeks. He had said then, "Are we clear?"

Fumbling for a response to Salina, Katherine said, "That we're clear. That everything is going to be okay."

"Why, yes, and that Jake will be safe also. I like Jake. He's a lot of fun."

Katherine cringed at the thought of something bad happening to Jake, then dismissed it. "I forgot to tell you why I came over."

"Yeah?"

Katherine pulled a bag of cat treats out of her coat's pocket. She opened the bag, then handed a treat to Wolfy.

"Mir-whoa," the skinny gray cat answered in a squeaky voice.

"You're welcome." Katherine tipped her head back and laughed.

Salina set Wolfy on the floor.

"Jake is fixing chili. Want to join us? The cats miss you, especially Abby."

"I miss Abby, too. Yes, I'd love to come over, but first I'll text my dad and let him know."

"Good. Say hello from me."

Katherine picked up Wolfy and began singing a tune she'd learned from Salina. "I'm holdin' a cat named Wolfy Joe. He looks like a werewolf, don't you know . . . "

The End

Dear Reader . . .

I love it when my readers write to me. If you'd like to email me about what you'd like to see in the next book, or just talk about your favorite scenes and characters, email me at: karenannegolden@gmail.com

Thank you so much for reading my book. I hope you enjoyed reading it as much as I did writing it. If you liked "*The Cats that Stole a Million*," I would be so thankful if you'd help others enjoy this book, too, by recommending it to your friends, family, and book clubs, and/or by writing a positive review on Amazon and/or Goodreads.

I love to post pictures of my cats on my Facebook pages, and would enjoy learning about your pets, as well.

Follow me @ https://www.facebook.com/karenannegolden

Amazon author page: http://tinyurl.com/mkmpg4d

Thanks again!

Karen

Acknowledgements

Thanks to my husband, Jeff, who is always the very first one to read my book.

Special thanks to Vicki Braun, my editor, who is a lot of fun to work with. Vicki also edited the first six books of *The Cats That . . .* Cozy Mystery series.

Also, thanks to philipsinc, my book cover designer.

Thank you to my friend, Ramona Kekstadt, and her dog Louie.

Thanks to my loyal readers, my family, and friends.

The Cats that . . . Cozy Mystery series would never be without the input from my furry friends.

The Cats that Surfed the Web

Book One in *The Cats that . . .* Cozy Mystery series

If you haven't read the first book, *The Cats that Surfed the Web*, you can download the Kindle version on Amazon: http://amzn.com/B00H2862YG Paperback is also available.

With over 455 Amazon positive reviews, "The Cats that Surfed the Web," is an action-packed, exhilarating read. When Katherine "Katz" Kendall, a career woman with cats, discovers she's the sole heir of a huge inheritance, she can't believe her good luck. She's okay with the conditions in the will: Move from New York City to the small town of Erie, Indiana, live in her great aunt's pink Victorian mansion, and take care of an Abyssinian cat. With her three Siamese cats and best friend Colleen riding shotgun, Katz leaves Manhattan to find a former housekeeper dead in the basement. There are people in the town who are furious that they didn't get the money. But who would be greedy enough to get rid of the rightful heir to take the money and run?

Four adventurous felines help Katz solve the crimes by mysteriously "searching" the Internet for clues. If you love cats, especially cozy cat mysteries, you'll enjoy this series.

The Cats that Chased the Storm

Book Two in *The Cats that . . .* Cozy Mystery series

The second book, *The Cats that Chased the Storm*, is also available on Kindle and in paperback. Amazon: http://amzn.com/B00IPOPJOU

It's early May in Erie, Indiana, and the weather has turned most foul. We find Katherine "Katz" Kendall, heiress to the Colfax fortune, living in a pink mansion, caring for her three Siamese and Abby the Abyssinian. Severe thunderstorms frighten the cats, but Scout is better than any weather app. A different storm is brewing, however, with a discovery that connects great-uncle William Colfax to the notorious gangster John Dillinger. Why is the Erie Historical Society so eager to get William's personal papers? Is the new man in Katherine's life a fortune hunter? Will Abra mysteriously reappear, and is Abby a magnet for danger?

A fast-paced whodunit, the second book in "The Cats that" series involves four extraordinary felines that help Katz unravel the mysteries in her life.

The Cats that Told a Fortune

Book Three in *The Cats that . . .* Cozy Mystery series

The third book, *The Cats that Told a Fortune*, is available on Kindle and in paperback. Amazon: http://amzn.com/B00MAAZ3ZU

With over 227 Amazon positive reviews, "The Cats that Told a Fortune" is an action-packed, exhilarating read. In the land of corn mazes and covered bridge festivals, a serial killer is on the loose. Autumn in Erie, Indiana means cool days of intrigue and subterfuge. Katherine "Katz" Kendall settles into her late great aunt's Victorian mansion with her five cats. A Halloween party at the mansion turns out to be more than Katz planned for. Meanwhile, she's teaching her first computer training class, and a serial killer is murdering young women. Along the way, Katz and her cats uncover important clues to the identity of the killer, and find out about Erie's local crime family . . . the hard way.

The Cats that Played the Market

Book Four in *The Cats that . . .* Cozy Mystery series

If you haven't read the fourth book, *The Cats that Played the Market*, you can download the Kindle version or purchase the paperback on Amazon at: http://amzn.com/B00Q71LBYA

If you love mysteries with cats, don't miss this action-packed page turner. A blizzard blows into Indiana, bringing gifts, gala events, and a ghastly murder to heiress Katherine "Katz" Kendall. It's Katherine's birthday, and she gets more than she bargains for when someone evil from her past comes back to haunt her. After all hell breaks loose at the Erie Museum's opening, Katherine and her five cats unwittingly stumble upon clues that help solve a mystery. But has Scout lost her special abilities? Or will Katz find that another one of her amazing felines is a super-sleuth?

With the cats providing clues, it's up to Katherine and her friends to piece together the murderous puzzle . . . before the town goes bust! With over 193 Amazon positive reviews, this thrilling, suspenseful read will keep you guessing until the last page.

The Cats that Watched the Woods

Book Five in *The Cats that . . .* Cozy Mystery series

If you haven't read the fifth book, *The Cats that Watched the Woods*, you can download the Kindle version or purchase the paperback on Amazon at: http://amzn.com/B00VKF9Q2M

What have the extraordinary cats of millionaire Katherine "Katz" Kendall surfed up now? "Idyllic vacation cabin by a pond stocked with catfish." It's July in Erie, Indiana, and steamy weather fuels the tension between Katz and her fiancé, Jake. Katz rents the cabin for a private getaway, though Siamese cats, Scout and Abra, demand to go along. How does a peaceful, serene setting go south in such a hurry? Is the terrifying man in the woods real, or is he the legendary ghost of Peace Lake? It's up to Katz and her cats to piece together the mysterious puzzle. The fifth book in the popular "The Cats that . . . Cozy Mystery" series is a suspenseful, thrilling ride that will keep you on the edge of your seat.

The Cats that Stalked a Ghost

Book Six in *The Cats that . . .* Cozy Mystery series

If you haven't read the sixth book, *The Cats that Stalked a Ghost*, you can download the Kindle version or purchase the paperback on Amazon at: http://amzn.com/B013VT44FI

If you love mysteries with cats, get ready for a thrilling, action-packed read that will keep you guessing until the very end. While Katherine and Jake are tying the knot at her pink mansion, a teen ghost has other plans, which shake their Erie, Indiana town to its core. How does a beautiful September wedding end in mistaken identity . . . and murder? What does an abandoned insane asylum have to do with a spirit that is haunting Katz? Colleen, a paranormal investigator at night and student by day, shows Katz how to communicate with ghosts. An arsonist is torching historic properties. Will the mansion be his next target? Ex-con Stevie Sanders and the Siamese play their own stalking games, but for different reasons. It's up to Katz and her extraordinary felines to solve two mysteries: one hot, one cold. Seal-point Scout wants a new adventure fix, and litter-mate Abra fetches a major clue that puts an arsonist behind bars. Enjoy this stand-alone novel, then learn more about these characters in their debut book, "The Cats that Surfed the Web." Amazon's bestselling author of "The Cats that . . . Cozy Mystery" series.

Made in the USA
San Bernardino, CA
10 April 2016